Illu
Franch

GW00859466

FOREWORD

Creativity and imagination are two of the greatest gifts that we possess. The deep mental capacity to transform our world with an idea. To bring joy, tears, love, light, and laughter with our essence. This book is dedicated to God because every good thing I have comes from my creator. It is also a tribute to my family for their constant love and support.

I started this journey twenty-five years ago when I first had the idea of a boy with magic glasses. The aim was to create a story that I could read to my children who were very small at the time. So, I wrote a few chapters and stopped. Little did I know that it would take me so long to start writing again, or that one of the children would grow up and be instrumental in getting it over the finish line.

Thank you Shanara for patiently going through the book with me and correcting my antediluvian English! Your input has been both inspirational and invaluable to this project.

Another person who has contributed to its completion is Francho. Her wonderful illustrations have literally brought the characters to life.

Initially, I was not going to write a foreword but realised that someone reading this book may have a project they started and failed to complete. Let me take this opportunity to encourage you to finish what you started, as art can be a great antidote to apathy.

I am extremely grateful to all those who have helped: my beloved wife Josephine for her continual encouragement, and Sandra G.

To
Aaron, Mark, Shanara, Teisha, Nia, Daniel and Kaiden.

CONTENTS

THE MEETING

GREGORY BUTLER lived with his mother Mavis in a small house on a quiet suburban street. His father had died when Gregory was just four years old, and he had no siblings. Indeed, his only friend was kept in a square tank on the bookshelf in his bedroom – a pet goldfish named Sharky.

Due to being rather small for a twelve-year-old, Gregory was often picked on at school. The fact that he had skinny little twiglet arms, bony legs, fuzzy ginger hair and wore thick obnoxious glasses *did not* help matters much either.

"Gregory, when are you leaving to go to the funfair? I don't want you getting back home too late!" shouted his mother impatiently from the hallway downstairs.

"I'm leaving now Mum!" he replied, grabbing some money off the table next to his bed and racing down the stairs. Mavis gave him a brief hug and ushered him out of the front door.

The bus stop was located a short distance from his home. Gregory had not been waiting long before he spotted the bus ambling towards him. He got on board and chose an isolated seat near the back. There were quite a few stops until he reached the fair, and Gregory started to think about his life at school.

His worst memory was when Ben had threatened him and flushed his head down the toilet for no reason at all. "*Let me go!*" he had cried out as his legs buckled, but Ben had just laughed and pushed him down further until his face smashed into the porcelain. Then Ben's gormless friends had joined him in the cruel mocking.

Gregory's thoughts were interrupted by the sound of the bus announcing his stop. He exited, walked further down the road, and made a right turn. The funfair rose proudly in front of him in all its dazzling glory.

He entered the long queue and paid the entrance fee. Once inside, Gregory went off to find the Bumper Cars, then the Big Wheel, and lastly took a jerky ride on Twister. By this point he had spent most of the money his mother had given him. Gregory was having such a fun day that he lost track of time.

It was getting dark and when he checked his phone to see what time it was, the battery was dead.

"Have you got the time please?" he asked a woman on his way to buy some candyfloss.

"Eight thirty,' she answered.

"Thanks," Gregory said. He put his dead phone back into his jacket and made his way to the exit.

"Roll up, roll up, come and see Mezra!" a strange voice yelled from behind him. When he turned around, he saw a clown standing in front of a huge silver and gold striped tent.

There was a large sign above the entrance that read: *THE GREAT MEZRA - THE MAGNIFICENT MAGICIAN.*

The tent looked inviting, and he joined the back of the queue that stretched around it. Standing in front of him was a man and his two children. He was tall and skinny, with large ears and high cheekbones. The children were short, fat and very noisy. The tall man reminded him of his father. *What would it be like if my dad was still alive?*

Suddenly, a cold hand covered his mouth and he found himself being dragged backwards behind the big tent. When they were out of sight the person aggressively spun him around. It was Ben.

"Give me your money," Ben demanded, and threw Gregory down onto the muddy ground. He instinctively touched his glasses to check that they were safe. "I haven't got any left," Gregory lied.

"I'll punch your lights out if you're lying," Ben threatened. Then, quicker than lightening, he put his hand inside Gregory's trouser pocket and pulled out a five-pound note.

"I warned you four eyes," he snarled, as he retracted his fist and punched him hard in the face. *Crack* was the sound his glasses made when they snapped, and Gregory's body landed on the muddy floor.

"Are you alright, lad?" a concerned voice asked. Gregory opened his eyes. His head was spinning, but he could just about make out the blurred wrinkly face of an old man in front of him. The man had a long grey beard and wore an odd hat.

"Yeah," he said groggily, "I'm alright."

The old man helped him to his feet and Gregory wiped away the blood trickling from a small cut at the side of his face. He straightened up his clothes and looked down at his dirty, mud-stained trousers.

"Where's my glasses?" he asked unsteadily.

"Capo has them," said the old man beckoning a clown over. It was the same clown that Gregory had seen earlier outside the tent. Capo handed the glasses to the old man, who looked down into his hand.

"These are not much use now," he said regretfully, as he stretched out his hand to give the broken glasses to Gregory.

"Thank you," Gregory said, and was just about to take them, when all at once he started to feel faint again and collapsed, falling to his knees.

"Help him up Capo," instructed the old man.

The clown picked him up and carried him to a rundown caravan at the back of the funfair. "Where shall I put him?" asked the clown once they were all inside.

"Over by the window," the old man answered.

Capo went and placed Gregory on a large patchwork cushion near the window, whilst the old man poured a drink into a crystal glass. He took it over to Gregory, who by this time was semi-conscious.

"Here drink this, it will make you feel better," said the old man passing him the glass. "Capo you may leave us now." The clown nodded curtly and left.

Now, usually, Gregory would never accept anything from a stranger, but he trusted this old man for some reason and drank. '*Yuk!*' he said, twisting his face in disapproval and almost spitting out the vile concoction. "This tastes disgusting and smells like my sweaty socks!"

The old man started to chuckle, "it appears to be working already."

He was right, as almost immediately after drinking it, Gregory's head felt much better, and he started to notice the things around him.

In the middle of the room there was a dusty, old wooden table. It had three large leather-bound books stacked on top of it.

On the wall opposite to where he was sitting was an antique Grandfather Clock. It did not appear to work as the pendulum was missing. Next to it was a portrait of a very beautiful lady in a lilac dress standing by a giant willow tree. The gilt-edged frame of the painting was covered in cobwebs.

"What's your name lad?" asked the old man as he walked to the centre of the room.

"Gregory sir, Gregory Butler".

"Okay Gregory, my name is Mezra. I am pleased to meet you." He gathered some official looking papers together and placed them in a cupboard

Gregory's mind was preoccupied. "Can I phone my mum please? My phone is dead, and she will be worried about me," he asked.

"Why certainly. You can use my phone." Mezra went over to a table and brought back an outdated-looking device.

"Thanks." He eyed the phone warily and dialled his mum's number. Gregory quickly explained what had happened with Ben and how a kind old man had come to his aid.

"My mum wants to talk to you," Gregory said, and handed the phone back.

Mezra spoke to Gregory's mum for a short while, then said goodbye to her. 'She is on her way to pick you up lad'.

"Thank you for helping sir. I really appreciate it." Gregory felt humbled by his kindness.

"Oh, don't mention it; you are a very brave boy."

"I don't feel brave," said Gregory, and burst into tears.

"No need to cry, lad, everything will be fine. Just wait and see; you will be okay." Mezra walked over to the corner of the room, stooped down, opened a large antique trunk, and rummaged through its contents. "Where are they? They are in here somewhere," he muttered to himself.

"What are you looking for?" Gregory asked, rubbing his eyes with a sleeve.

"Aha, here they are!" Mezra took out a small brown box from the trunk.

He walked over to Gregory. "Yes, indeed, these will cheer you up." Mezra smiled warmly and gave him the box.

"What's this, sir?" Gregory asked excitedly.

"It is the key to an adventure," Mezra replied.

Gregory looked closely at the box. It was roughly the same size as a pencil case and made from wood. On top of the lid were some strange symbols and engravings of birds.

"Do you know what those pictures are Gregory?" Mezra pointed to the top of the box.

"Yes sir, I do. They are called 'hydro-giblets.' We learnt about them at school," he answered confidently.

"No, not hydro-giblets, *hieroglyphics*," Mezra said laughing. "It was the type of writing used in ancient Egypt."

While Gregory was studying the box, Mezra took one of the dusty leather books off the table and placed it inside the trunk.

"What does it say?" asked Gregory inquisitively, running his short fingers along the hieroglyphics.

Mezra closed the trunk firmly and looked Gregory straight in the eye. "This is no ordinary box," he paused, "inside are magic glasses that can change your life forever. They can make you see things which are unseen, and take you on wondrous journeys to faraway places."

He opened the box to reveal a strange pair of glasses. "They are thousands of years old and extremely powerful." The old man's face had a serious expression that Gregory had not seen on it before.

Mezra closed the trunk firmly and looked Gregory straight in the eye. "This is no ordinary box," he paused, "inside are magic glasses that can change your life forever. They can make you see things which are unseen, and take you on wondrous journeys to faraway places."

Mezra closed the trunk firmly and looked Gregory straight in the eye. "This is no ordinary box," he paused, "inside are magic glasses that can change your life forever. They can make you see things which are unseen, and take you on wondrous journeys to faraway places."

He opened the box to reveal a strange pair of glasses. "They are thousands of years old and extremely powerful."

The old man's face had a serious expression that Gregory had not seen on it before.

Gregory stared at the box open-mouthed. "If you want to be the guardian of the magic glasses you must first make a pledge," Mezra continued.

"What pledge?" asked Gregory eagerly.

"A serious pledge, lad, and one that must be made truthfully."

"I will make the pledge. What do I have to say?" Gregory asked eagerly.

"You must be one hundred percent sure lad. These magic glasses come with a great responsibility," Mezra warned.

"That's okay, I can do it! My mum is always telling me I should be more responsible."

The old man laughed out loud. "I do not think that your mother meant this type of responsibility, lad. You must be sure before you make the pledge. There will be no turning back once you begin."

"I am sure. Please, I must make the pledge,' implored Gregory.

"Very well then. You must repeat the words inscribed inside of the box." Then Mezra spoke the words and Gregory nervously repeated them.

"*I will read a book on a full moon, be carried away to a new world, I will not return until my work is done, evil has perished, and goodness has won.*"

"Now, there are a few things that I must tell you before you go," Mezra said in a serious tone. "The glasses will only work on a full moon. When you read a book, you will be into the story that you are reading."

He sat down next to the trunk and continued to explain. "Listen closely to me Gregory. It is very important that you never remove the glasses for more than twelve hours in the book realm. For if you do, you will immediately be returned to the place where you started reading the book. The pledge will be broken, and the power of the magic glasses lost forever." Mezra stared at Gregory as though he were trying to read his mind.

"Do you understand Gregory?"

"I think so," he slowly replied.

Gregory stared into the box, his heart beating rapidly in his chest. There they were! The glasses were transparent and resembled swimming goggles, but they were not rubber. The magic glasses appeared to be made from a fabric material. There was a dial on the bridge of the nose and a switch on the side of the right lens resembling an on/off button.

"They don't look like they can do magic," Gregory said in a disappointed tone.

"Never judge a book by its cover. There is much more to those glasses than meets the eye." Mezra had a huge smile and looked as though he wanted to laugh.

"I don't mean to sound ungrateful," he said, taking a closer look at the glasses. "This all seems like a dream to me. Like I will wake up any time now. Is it really true?"

"Absolutely, you see the dial on the bridge and the switch on the side?"

"Yes." Gregory responded, eyeing them both carefully.

"Familiarise yourself with them Gregory," Mezra said thoughtfully. "They will do nothing for you now, but once you enter into a story, they will be of great use to you. If you click down the switch on the side, you will become completely invisible, and if you click it up you will be seen by all."

"Wow, I can become invisible," Gregory exclaimed and sprung off the patchwork cushion with enthusiasm. "Down - invisible: up – visible. Cool, that is easy to remember. What does the dial in the middle do?"

"There are eleven settings on the dial, lad. Number one is normal and will keep you the same. All other numbers will bring special powers."

"That is great! What special things will I be able to do?" Gregory asked.

"You will have to find that out for yourself. Experiment with the other numbers once you are inside the book. However, in order to protect yourself and others, you must time when you change the settings carefully," Mezra instructed cryptically.

"Why are you giving them to me? You don't even know me."

"Our meeting today was predestined. The Book Champions were decided long ago by the Council of Protectors. It was fate that brought you here tonight. The magic glasses are meant to be with you, and I know that you will take good care of them."

"Oh yes, I will definitely take care of the glasses," Gregory promised.

They spent some time discussing the powers of the magic glasses, with Gregory asking question after question. Mezra told him that he would need many qualities to successfully complete tasks in the book realm:

"You will need strength of character and faith to achieve victory. The Book Champion must also possess a strong will and promote kindness in all their works. In all things, use good judgement and wisdom. Lastly, never fight the spirit of your love, imagination and intelligence."

Gregory tried his best to remember everything Mezra told him. There was a knock on the door of the caravan. Mezra opened it to reveal Gregory's mum wearing a long green coat. "Hello, my name is Mavis. I am Gregory's mum," she extended her hand for Mezra to take.

"I am Mezra. Pleased to meet you. Do come in."

Mavis entered the caravan and saw Gregory sitting by the window. He got up and ran over to give her a big hug. "Are you alright, Son? Is anything broken?" Mavis felt his arms and legs for injuries.

"I'm okay, Mum," he said smiling at her reassuringly.

"What is wrong with these thugs?" she asked in anger. "Are you sure you can't remember what they looked like?"

"No Mum, it happened too fast." Gregory did not want to tell her that it had been Ben who had attacked him.

"Okay, come on then, let us go home," she said.

On the way out she thanked Mezra once again for his kindness. As they said their farewells, Gregory stood there wondering if the magic glasses were real, or just a story that the magician had told to cheer him up.

"Mum, I badly need to use the toilet."

"It is just through there on the right-hand side," said Mezra.

"Thanks," Gregory said, and made his way to the toilet. Once inside he put on the 'magic glasses' and looked at himself in the mirror. "I look like an idiot," he muttered, quietly laughing as he put them back in their case.

"Are you ready now?" Mavis asked when Gregory appeared back at the front door.

"You are forgetting these, lad," Mezra said as he held out his hand.

Gregory looked and was astonished to see the glasses Ben had broken. They were now perfectly intact. A shocked Gregory took the glasses and put them on. He realised that everything Mezra had told him was true.

THE TASK

Gregory woke up early in the morning and looked out of his bedroom window. The pink roses his mother had planted in the back garden were in full bloom, swaying gently in the breeze.

Two weeks had passed from the day he met Mezra, and there was finally going to be a full moon. It had been the longest fortnight of his life. Gregory had not been able to sleep properly since the meeting. He tingled in anticipation of trying out the magic glasses.

Gregory carried out his daily routine as usual. He fed Sharky, had a quick shower, got dressed and then ate his favourite breakfast - a bowl of cereal.

After he had eaten, Gregory went into the garden shed to get his red mountain bike.

"Where are you off to, sweetheart?" Mavis asked out of the kitchen window as he opened the gate and pushed the bike through. She had a broad smile on her face that highlighted her soft round cheeks.

"Just to the park, Mum!" he shouted, then mounted the saddle and set off on his ride.

"Remember we are going to the cinema later. Don't be too long!" Mavis called out after him as she waved him goodbye.
'I won't be late!" he yelled back in response, pedalling off at speed and nearly clipping a lamp post as he briefly lost his balance.

Gregory had been pestering his mother with the same question at least once a day ever since he had got the magic glasses. "When is the next full moon, Mum?"

"Not again," Mavis would groan, "are you a werewolf or something? Why don't you just check on your phone?"
Gregory had lied and said that he was interested in astrology.

It got to the point where Mavis was so fed up with him that she bought a calendar, and marked with a cross all the dates on which a full moon would appear.

Gregory decided to ride down to Bushy Park - the place where the funfair had been. It seemed only right that he went back to where Mezra had given him the glasses on that special day. He had returned to the park a day after he met *Mezra the Magnificent*, but to his disappointment, the funfair had moved on. Gregory had even asked his mother if she had taken down Mezra's number. She gave it to him, but whenever he tried to call, it the user was unavailable.

When he arrived at Bushy Park, he quickly found the place where Mezra's caravan had stood, and rested down on the grass with his bike beside him. Gregory searched his memory trying to recall every word that Mezra had spoken to him that night. *He told me I must be prepared.*

Ever since that night he had somehow felt different. He did not feel weak and pathetic anymore. Indeed, for some reason, even Ben had been leaving him alone lately. It seemed as if the magic glasses had changed his life before he had even worn them.

As he sat there, thinking on the grass, along came a slightly built man walking a large, boisterous dog on a lead. He was being pulled, left, right and centre by the hound. It was running with great keenness from tree to bench, and back to tree.

All the time, sniffing and barking every few yards or so. The owner was clearly out of his depth and did not have the dog fully under control.

'Wait, Benton! Stop pulling me!" bellowed the owner.

Gregory stood up and picked up his bike. He sensed danger and did not want to be a sitting target for the dog. Then the expected happened! Benton pulled the lead from its owner's hand and bounded towards Gregory at great speed, barking its head off.

"Stop Benton! Get back here!" the man shouted after it, but it carried on regardless.

When the dog was almost upon him, Gregory looked it in the eye and said firmly, "Benton sit." Incredibly that is exactly what Benton did. The dog immediately stopped running and sat down.

Gregory picked up the lead and walked the dog over to the owner. He was pushing the bike with one hand, and leading the dog in the other. For the first time in his life, Gregory felt empowered, and he liked the feeling a lot.

"Thank you. I am very sorry the lead just slipped through my hand," the man said apologetically, as Gregory handed Benton over to him.

"No problem," said Gregory, patting Benton on the head and rubbing his fur. The owner smiled gratefully and walked away. Gregory returned to his position on the grass and sat down.

After a couple of hours at Bushy Park the sky turned cloudy, and he rode home. Later that afternoon, his mother took him to the cinema. She bought some popcorn along with fizzy drinks, and they settled into their seats to watch the latest sci-fi movie. They hadn't been to the cinema in a long while, and both really enjoyed the film.

When they came out, it was already dark. He looked up into the sky to see if there was a full moon, but the sky was full of clouds, and he could not see it. "I wonder if the glasses will work if you can't see the moon properly," he muttered under his breath.

"What's that, sweetheart?" Mavis asked.

"Nothing, Mum," he said nervously. "I was remembering a good scene from the movie."

On the way home they stopped off at a Chinese restaurant. *What a great way to get ready for an adventure*, Gregory said to himself, as he bit into a tasty spring roll. His mother was sitting on the opposite side of the table eating a seafood dish. Mavis loved seafood as she grew up in Swanage (a small town by the sea), and both of her brothers were fishermen. After finishing their meal, his mum called a taxi. They arrived home at around 9pm.

'Would you like some tea?' Mavis asked.

"No thanks, I'm full up. I think I will go straight to bed. Goodnight, Mum." Gregory zoomed up the stairs, like a rocket off a launch pad, to his bedroom.

As he opened the door, his mum called out, "Goodnight, Son, and stop running up the stairs!"

Gregory entered his bedroom and rushed over to the fish tank. "Hey Sharky, it's time for action." He looked out of the bedroom window at the night sky. The full moon was still hidden behind the clouds.

"I'm going to test them anyway." Gregory sighed and sprinkled some fish food in the tank.

His mouth was dry as he went over and took his backpack from the wardrobe. He opened it up for a final check. Inside, were all the things that he thought could be needed in the book realm. There was a long rope, six candles, four lighters, a torch, eight bars of chocolate, two fizzy drinks, a pellet gun with ammunition, a Swiss Army Knife, and much more…

The last item he placed in was his ebony harmonica. His father had bought it as a gift before he died, and it was very special to him. *That should be everything*, he thought, as he put on the backpack and strapped it up tightly.

Gregory carefully took the magic glasses from out of its secret hiding place under the wardrobe. Then grabbed a book from the shelf and sat down on the edge of his bed. His hands were shaking as he removed the glasses from their case. Gregory studied them to make sure the switch on the side was pressed down. He also double-checked that the dial in the middle was on setting number one.

Very slowly, he put on the glasses and looked at the book in his hand. It was titled '*The Kingdom of Rage*'. He had purchased it the week before from his favourite bookshop. As he sat there nervously, Gregory was overwhelmed by a sense of panic, and, dropping the book, he rushed to the bathroom and promptly threw up.

On returning to the bedroom, he sat back down on the bed and picked the book up once more. Gregory anxiously glanced over at Sharky, and then said the words that Mezra had taught him:

"I will read a book on a full moon. Be carried away to a new world. I will not return until my work is done, evil has perished, and goodness has won."

He warily opened the book and started to read. "This is the story of...." Suddenly, there was a flash of blinding light and the white pages turned black. The words typed in black ink became a startling white. Then the whole book changed into a multi-coloured cascade of ink as the words swirled off the pages.

WOW! Gregory was in the book ascending a star-spangled spiral cylinder. His eyes were tightly closed when he was alerted by the sound of loud bells and fast-beating music. He could feel his heart racing, and the hair at the back of his neck stood on end.

Then, quicker than you can say, '*books are better than television,*' he landed with a thud on the ground. Fortunately, it was on very soft sand: but unfortunately for him he landed face down. There was fine sand: in his mouth and stuck up his nostrils. "Where am I?" he spluttered.

He looked around at his new surroundings. *What a strange place this is,* he thought. Gregory was on a beach; but this was like no other place he had seen before. The sand consisted of purple and yellow polka dots, the sea was light green, and the sky was a very strange, luminous, lilac colour. There were huge red mountains all around that seemed to go on for many miles. Unlike the beaches his mother used to take him to on vacation, this beach did not smell salty. Instead, it had a sweet, sugary fragrance.

Gregory checked that his backpack was secure and waded into the sea. He bent over, cupping his hands, and scooping up some of the light green liquid. *What a delightful smell,* he thought, holding the liquid to his nose. Although the substance smelt good, he did not want to taste it just in case it was poisonous.

Then, without warning, his right shoulder was gripped by a giant hairy claw. It was razor sharp and cut into his backpack. "*AARGH,*" he yelled, as he was carried up high into the lilac sky. He looked up and was horrified to see a flying monster holding him. It looked like a big hairy whale with the head of a snake.

Too scared to continue staring at the creature, he looked downwards instead. Gregory was sailing high above the red mountains that he had just been admiring from the safety of the beach. Everything looked blurry from this distance.

Hang on a minute, how did the creature see me? He felt the switch on the side of the glasses, and it was up. It must have changed when he impacted the sand entering the book realm. Gregory knew that he was probably on his way to be gobbled up by a nest full of baby monsters and had an idea. He reached into his backpack and searched around until he found one of the lighters. Then he adjusted the flame setting on the side to maximum, and, *flick, flick,* it was alight.

He placed the flame on the creature's hairy claw. The hair instantly caught fire, and, with a loud *hiss,* the Snagon released its grip and let him go.

Gregory landed on his back in a lake. To his surprise he did not sink, but sprung off its surface straight back into the air. He bounced several more times on the lake, each time getting lower and lower, before finally coming to a stop. Gregory lay there for a while on his back trying to get his senses together. After a short time, he heard a weird noise and quickly sat up. He looked up into the sky to see if the monster was returning to finish him off, but there was nothing in sight. The noise grew louder, and he frantically looked around.

Across the lake there were four figures running towards him, waving their hands in the air. As they drew closer, he realised that they were not running at all, but were floating over the lake like they were on a hover-board.

They all were at least seven feet tall. *What kind of beings are these?*

Gregory remembered the switch on the side of the glasses and clicked it down to become invisible.

He sat frozen to the spot in fear as they drew near. Gregory saw that the beings all had three legs, pale yellow skin, and flowing dark hair. They were speaking in a language he could not understand.

In no time at all, they were right next to him, standing together in heated debate, rather confused, and flapping their hands around. The glasses worked; he could not be seen by them. He stood up extremely slowly and cautiously started to move away. After he took about ten steps, one of them turned around and looked over in his direction. They had heard him. The strange beings started to float towards him, and goose bumps rose on his skin. In panic, he grabbed the dial in the middle of the magic glasses and twisted it.

Gregory began to rapidly decrease in size and the world around him grew bigger. He stopped shrinking when he became ten centimetres tall. The figures looked enormous. One of them was directly on top of him, feeling the air with their long hands, but of course, finding nothing.

He walked away as fast as his miniature feet could carry him and stopped about a metre from where the beings were. Gregory watched their looks of confusion as they talked loudly in a foreign language. A few minutes of intense conversation continued between them before they hovered off, heading back in the same direction from which they came.

He waited until they were completely out of sight and then felt the dial in the middle of the glasses to see what setting it was on. It was number two.

I need to test the rest of the settings, he said to himself. However, he was still standing in the middle of the Spongey Lake. Concerned that one of the settings would do something crazy and draw attention, he decided to find a bit of cover over by the red mountains.

Before he set off, he twisted the dial back to number one. Quick as a flash, Gregory went back to his normal size, his body making a weird high-pitched noise as he grew.

Then he headed towards the large set of red mountains in the distance. To his amusement, thirty minutes of bouncy walking followed.

He reached the edge of the lake and in the distance saw a cat-like animal with its back towards him. It was quite animated, bending down and making noises into a large crater.

As Gregory moved closer the animal turned around and sniffed the air as if it had sensed his presence.

It was light brown in colour, with the head of a cat, and the body of a kangaroo. The creature had human-like arms, and hands with claws instead of paws. On its face were very long whiskers and a red button nose.

Gregory stood perfectly still. It was holding a large javelin; and he did not want to be skewered like barbecued beef.

Then a painful howl came from the crater that sounded like a wounded animal. Instantly, the creature with the javelin returned its attention back to whatever was in the crater.

What is going on? Gregory asked himself. He guardedly made his way over to the hole, keeping a safe distance away from the creature. When he looked over the edge, he saw another cat-like creature at the bottom, limping around.

They were talking to each other, but Gregory could not understand them. Both made high-pitched yelps like small dogs barking. He knew that the one in the hole was hurt, as it was whimpering.

At that point he was not sure what to do. He had no option but to try another setting on the glasses. Setting one was normal size and setting two was shrinking.

Gregory turned the dial to number three. He suddenly understood the communication between both animals. *This is absolutely amazing, I have a translator,* he thought. Gregory twisted the dial back and forth from setting one to three a couple of times to hear the yelps turn into words and vice versa.

The creature at the bottom of the hole was shouting up. "What will we do? My foot is broken." It looked extremely worried.

"I don't know. There is no way I can get down there," the other creature shouted. "We need some help. I will go back and get some."

"No, don't do that. It will take more than a day for you to return! I will not survive," said the creature in the hole panicking.

"Calm down, Yord. We need help, brother. It will not take me a day to return; I will be back in no time.

What other choice do we have?" responded the creature at the top of the hole.

"I am injured. What if a Snagon comes? I will be finished!" said Yord, growing increasingly upset.

"Trust me, brother, you will be alright. Just take it easy. You are not helping matters."

"Trust you? You always say that Droll, and we keep getting into trouble. Father told us never to come out here alone, but you insisted." Yord scoffed, grimacing in pain.

"Stop whining, I am sick of staying in Geba; it is so boring,"

"I would rather be back in Geba than stuck in this hole," said Yord. "Are you listening to me Droll?"

"Yes, I can hear what you say. Now let me think," Droll said, as he held is chin in his hand.

Gregory wanted to help, but did not want to startle them in case he was impaled by the javelin, so he grabbed it out of the creature's hand. Droll was in utter shock to see his weapon floating in the air.

"I want to help you. Don't be afraid," Gregory said reassuringly in their language. The creature looked even more surprised.

"Who said that?" Droll looked left and right, searching for the source of the voice.

"You cannot see me, but I am right in front of you, holding your spear."

Droll was afraid and stumbled backwards, almost falling down the hole himself. Gregory grabbed him by the arm and pulled him away from the edge.

"What are you?" Droll asked in fear.

"I am a boy," answered Gregory.

"What is a boy?"

"No time to explain now. I think that I came across a Snagon earlier and I don't want a reunion. Let's get Yord out of the hole."

"Sounds like a good idea, boy, but how are we going to do that?"

"I will use my glasses," answered Gregory, and he turned the dial to setting number four; but nothing happened, except he could no longer understand what Droll was saying; it just sounded like yelps again. Then he tried level five, and again nothing happened. Next, he went to level six. Still nothing.

In frustration, he twisted the dial all the way to the final setting - number eleven. Then his body started to feel as if it was being pulled apart as he grew bigger and bigger, until he was fifty metres high.

He looked down to see Droll and Yord below. They were so tiny to him! Gregory bent over and put his giant hand into the hole and gently picked up Yord. Then he placed him carefully next to Droll at the top of the hole.

As Gregory straightened up, he felt a sense of pride. His joy was soon cut short, when out of the blue he was hit by a blow to the back of his massive head, and he fell unconscious to the floor.

THE PROPHECY

King Beserk sat menacingly on his large granite throne in the centre of Korfe Castle. Sadly, the once beautiful throne room was now a dreary and dilapidated place.

In front of him were four bedraggled prisoners on their knees cowering, awaiting their fate. King Berserk was a complete beast in every sense of the word. More than eight feet tall and very hairy. His jagged teeth jutted out from his lower jaw, and were so long that they scraped the tip of his big snout.

Hung around his thick neck was the Amulet of Sini. King Beserk had removed it from the dead body of Warlow - a master wizard. It provided protection against all types of sorcery and the King never took it off. On his left wrist he wore the dreaded Band of Torment, which he used mercilessly to inflict unimaginable pain on anyone who crossed him.

"You are here before the King charged with failing to supply the correct amount of Akiti," said Paro, the palace prosecutor to the prisoners. "What do you have to say to the King? Speak up while you still can, you scum," he demanded, running out of breath.

The four prisoners started whining and pleading for their lives. "My Lord, I beg of you. I have a husband and children. It was impossible to do what you asked. There is not enough Akiti left in the land," one of the prisoners grovelled.

"It is true, Your Majesty. We had to go into the land of the Feliroo. They were mighty and overpowered us, so we withdrew. We would have surely perished if we did not retreat," another of the prisoners chipped in.

"What!" Berserk shouted, as he raised his hand shaking the Band of Torment. It began to glow red, and everyone was completely terrified. The prisoners started to scream and shudder on the floor in excruciating pain.

"You dare to tell me you were defeated by those vermin." The King stared furiously at the prisoners, his red eyes bulging in anger. They all continued to shake and wail horrendously.

"Screen!" Berserk shouted, and at once Paro put up a shield between the prisoners and the King. The four prisoners exploded into thousands of pieces and their body parts splattered.

Several guards sprang into action, frantically cleaning the mess off the floor and walls. The prisoners green gooey blood and pieces of flesh were wiped away in seconds. Paro lowered the shield, then went before the throne, and bowed. "Your Majesty, the Akiti stocks are diminishing. What shall we do?" The King sat back on the throne with a crazed look in his eyes and took a slow sip of his drink. "More Akiti!" he screamed at Paro, and angrily threw his golden plate onto the floor.

Paro gestured to a guard, who scurried off to get the food before he felt the wrath of the King.

"Your Majesty, what is to be done? We will soon run out of food," Paro said apprehensively.

"Silence!" roared the King as he looked to the left of the throne room.

In the far corner stood a life-sized statue of his dead wife Queen Flora. Berserk groaned as he stood up and walked slowly over to it. He pressed his mouth close to its ear and whispered. "Do you hear, my love? I must break my promise to you."

There was an uneasy silence amongst all the guards present.

Meanwhile, the guard that had gone to get the Akiti was in the outer chamber returning with the food. A hologram of Mediana the Sorceress appeared before him. She was not allowed to go directly to the King without notice, so would send messages through his guards.

"Tell the King I need to see him urgently," her snake-like voice echoed off the walls.

The guard stopped in his tracks. "Right away,' he said and continued back to the throne room.

"My Lord," said the guard, and bowed before the King with an overflowing tray of freshly prepared Akiti. The King signalled him forward. He passed the food to King Berserk who immediately started stuffing his face like a hungry pig.

The guard stood there and waited for the King to finish eating the Akiti so he could tell him about Mediana. It was not wise to give him any news before or during his meal as the reaction was usually fatal for the messenger.

Berserk finished devouring the Akiti in a matter of seconds as his sharp teeth tore it apart and he swallowed the flesh in large gulps.

"My Lord," said the guard quietly.

"What is it?" asked the King, impatiently tapping his fingers on the side of the throne.

"Mediana is here, Your Majesty. She needs to speak to you urgently."

"Send her in at once!" King Beserk ordered.

"Yes, my Lord," the guard turned and ran back out.

Mediana approached the King, her head bowed down in obedience and fear. She was the daughter of the late Warlow the wizard and obligated by tradition to serve whoever wore the Amulet of Sini.

"What do you want witch?" asked the King impatiently as he shuffled himself on the throne.

"He is here my Lord," Mediana said, still looking down on the ground.

The King immediately knew whom she was referring to. He put both of his huge hands on his head in exasperation. "Everyone out!"

Paro and all the guards quickly left the throne room leaving King Berserk and Mediana alone. "Where is he?" asked the King.

"I don't know exactly. I only know that he is in the kingdom, my Lord."

King Beserk slumped back. "What do you mean? Show me what you have seen," he said in an agitated voice.

Mediana waved her hands over the palace floor in a circular motion and smoke began to rise from the grey granite. An image gradually appeared in the smoke, and they were seeing through the eyes of the Snagon that had attacked Gregory.

They watched it snatch Gregory up in its claws, soaring into the sky. Then they heard the Snagon shriek in pain, look down

at its flaming leg and drop him back onto the Spongey Lake. The image began to fade, and the smoke departed.

"How long ago did this happen?" asked the King, gravely concerned.

"Not long ago, my Lord."

"Manaso!" Beserk screamed.

Into the room came a mighty minotaur, with a heavy marble club in its hand. Manaso weighed so much that the room shook with every step.

"Bring Skrimp, and tell the Special Guard that the one we have been waiting for has arrived," the King commanded. Manaso nodded his head and left.

"What of the Nactu? Any news?" King Berserk asked Mediana with a growl.

"No, my Lord, we have excavated nearly all the burial ground in Tevro and still have not found it. The guardians of the Nactu have hidden it well," she said, her eyes still focussed on the ground.

'I need it now!" thundered the King lividly, as he leapt off the throne.

"What do you want me to do, my Lord?" Mediana asked fretfully.

"Find out where Fire Head is and bring me the Nactu!"

"At once, Your Majesty." She bowed and her hologram disappeared in a flash of fire.

Once alone, King Berserk pushed the throne across the floor, and opened a secret chamber underneath one of the granite tiles. Inside was a ragged black box.

He opened the lid and looked at the contents, smiling slowly and starting to cackle.

The King could hear the thundering footsteps of the minotaur getting closer. He closed the lid and put it back in its secret place, quickly pushing the throne back into position.

There was a knock on the throne room door. "Enter!" said the King. Manaso, Skrimp and the seven Special Guard all walked into the room.

Skrimp was King Berserk's most trusted and loyal servant. She was an extremely strong and fearsome warrior, deadly accurate with a Drad – a type of crossbow. The weapon was kept concealed under her kimono-like robe. She was not one of the Special Guard, but an unrivalled assassin.

"My Lord, we are at your service," Skrimp said hurriedly. "I came as soon as possible. Are the Mellows going to attack?" she asked hopefully.

Skrimp was itching to go to war with the Mellows as she hated them. They were responsible for the destruction of her entire family. King Berserk had saved her from certain death and brought her to live with him.

"No, my servant. I need you for another task."

He beckoned Skrimp to him and she humbly bowed before his throne. King Berserk placed his hand lovingly on her head.

"There is an intruder in our kingdom who must be found and destroyed," he said.

"A single intruder?" she asked, rather puzzled.

"Yes, one intruder, but he cannot be underestimated. He poses a serious threat to us and is somewhere near the Spongey Lake."

"I will take care of him for you. One intruder is like a fly compared to your greatness my King. He does not deserve the attention of your Special Guard my Lord. Please allow me to go alone and kill him for you."

King Berserk smiled with a devious look on his face. "Your loyalty is admirable, tiny one."

He looked around at his Special Guard. "This is how a true warrior should be. She has a brave heart. Follow her example during this mission and you will be great in the Kingdom of Rage."

"My Lord, I beg of you to let me go alone. I will not fail you," Skrimp repeated.

The King's face changed from joy to anger as he shooed her away with his hand. "I said no! Now go with the others and find Fire Head. Do not question me on the matter again!"

"Yes, my Lord." Skrimp's face had gone quite red with embarrassment. It was not a good idea to question the King when he was like this, so she and the seven Special Guard left the throne room.

Once they were outside, Opuc, one of the seven, said loudly. "The King is afraid of one intruder! What is wrong with him? His paranoia has reached new levels," Opuc laughed a moment before an arrow from Skrimp's Drad pierced his heart.

She looked at the others. "Nobody mocks my Lord and lives." The guards left their dead comrade lying on the floor and made their way outside of the castle. Now there were six Special Guard.

Meanwhile, deep down in the castle dungeons, a jailer was walking with a tray of food in his hands. He passed a large cell, full of prisoners. There were no bars or doors; the thirty prisoners were kept in by an invisible force field. As the guard trudged past, the prisoners began to shout.

"Give us some of that food!" screamed one of them.

"Let us out! We have done nothing wrong!" cried another, and threw an object at the guard. The item instantly caught fire as it hit the force field and bounced back on to the prisoner, setting his clothes ablaze.

All the other inmates rushed to put him out with their blankets as he screamed in agony. The guard continued walking, the tray in his hands.

Once he had passed the cell, he turned left into a dimly candle-lit corridor and eventually came to a large oak door. Placing the tray down on the ground, he took out a bunch of keys and opened it.

Although the room was big enough to hold ten people, it had a sole occupant who was sitting reading a book at a desk in the corner.

"Your Majesty, I have brought you food and wonderful news!" said the guard grinning. "He is here!"

The weathered face of the man at the desk looked up and returned the smile. "It is time to prepare. Are the forces ready Latip?" said King Cordial, the dethroned, rightful ruler of the palace.

"Yes, Your Majesty, they are gathering. The prophecy will soon be fulfilled, and we will finally rid ourselves of these evil usurpers," Latip said, openly bursting with joy as he put the tray on the desk.

"We still have a hard fight ahead of us, but this castle and kingdom shall be ours once again. Thanks be to God," said Cordial.

"It has been so long, Your Majesty. My heart bleeds when I think about what has happened to our people and this land."

King Cordial smiled sadly, "we cannot dwell on the past my friend. We Mellows have all lost very much, but now we need to focus on the future." The King stood up, opened his arms wide and hugged Latip.

"You have such wisdom my King, and a heart full of compassion and hope."

"I would not have made it this far without your help old friend," the King sighed. "Now tell me, how are your children?" "Caria has learnt how to ride a Ranty, and Marla is looking forward to going to school when the magra returns." Latip answered proudly.

"Riding a Ranty already! That is very impressive for one so young," King Cordial replied.

"Her mother would have been so proud of her. It is a shame she is not here to see it." Latip's eyes saddened as he spoke.

"Where is the Fire Head?"

"He was seen at Spongey Lake, my King. Berserk has sent his Special Guard to hunt him down."

"Then we must find him first Latip."

"The Mellow Patrol are searching for him as we speak. As soon as I have any news, I will let you know at once Your Majesty," promised Latip.

"That is good. Today is a day of hope. Now come, let me tell you my plan to take back the castle." King Cordial sat back down on the chair. "We must talk to King Griscat and ask for the help of the Feliroo."

Latip was shocked by the King's words. "Your Majesty, King Griscat will never join with us to fight against Berserk."

"That is incorrect, Latip. It will not be easy to convince him, but it is part of the prophecy that the Feliroo will be fighting by our side when we take back our land."

Latip did not look convinced.

"I know, my King, but a Feliroo never breaks his word, and King Griscat swore to Queen Flora on her death bed that he would not fight against Berserk."

"Have a little faith, my friend. After all, the Fire Head is here in the kingdom. Is that not a clear sign that the prophecy will be fulfilled? Let us prepare ourselves for what is about to come!"

THE SEARCH

Gregory woke up next to the crater where the injured Yord had been trapped. His right cheek was pressed down in the dust, and the back of his head ached. As he opened his eyes wider, Gregory's heart sank, and he sat up quickly.

There was a Snagon right beside him and, full of dread at the thought of what might happen next, he took a large gulp of air and studied the beast.

"*Phew!*" It lay completely still on the ground, so the Snagon was either dead or unconscious.

What is going on? Gregory asked himself, trying to work out what happened. It must have flown into him because he was invisible. Delicately, he touched the back of his head and found a large tender lump caused by the collision.

There was no sign of Droll or Yord, and Gregory wondered where they were.

He pondered what to do next, turning the dial in the middle of the magic glasses to setting number one. This decreased him back to normal size. Then Gregory made himself visible. He still had on his backpack which grew and shrunk, depending on the magic glasses' settings.

"I am starving," Gregory said as he removed the backpack and opened it. He pulled out a bar of chocolate and took a big bite. Gregory sat there a while enjoying his sweet. However, his chocolate break did not last long as it was interrupted by the sound of voices yelling in the distance.

Across the lake were the same four figures he had seen earlier. They floated towards him, waving their hands in the air like over enthusiastic cheerleaders. This time he was not going to disappear without trying something else first. He put down the bar of chocolate and turned the dial to number three so he could translate their voices.

"Please don't go. We are not going to harm you!" shouted the smallest of the creatures. The sound reverberated around the Spongey Lake. Then another creature yelled, "we are here to help you!"

He sat there next to his chocolate bar, too tired to do anything else. The figures got nearer, and their sounds got louder and louder as they drew close to him.

"How did you escape the Snagon?" asked the tallest one. "No one has ever been able to escape its clutches!"

Before Gregory had a chance to answer, the creature asked, "Did you kill it?" It sounded excited at the thought.

"No, I think it is only knocked out," he said finishing off the chocolate and putting the wrapper in his pocket. Even in the book realm, Gregory wanted to take care of the environment.

"You speak our language!" exclaimed the creature in astonishment. They all looked at each other impressed with his fluency and pronunciation. Their dialect was very complicated, and it was rare they came across a foreigner who could communicate with them.

"Well... yes," he said, and stood up with the backpack in his hand, still a bit unsteady after the collision with the Snagon. *This getting hit in the head thing is becoming too frequent,* he thought to himself.

"You must kill the Snagon now," said the figure, pointing a pale finger towards the beast. "We will take its head back to the camp so our people can rejoice." The others nodded in agreement.

"I am not cutting off any creature's head." Gregory said in disgust as he put the backpack on again. "That's horrible! Let's just leave it and go!"

"You are meant to be a hero, but talk like a coward," said one of the figures, angrily. "Are you here to help us or not?"

She was playing with a gadget in her hand. It was a long thin metal tube with little lights on the side. It reminded Gregory of a drinking straw.

"Cease, Private." said the tallest one sternly. She wore the same tunic as the rest of them, but with different coloured sleeves. Gregory thought that maybe it was to show that she was of a higher rank.

"Yes, Captain Placid," said the other creature, humbly backing down. The captain also drew out a metal tube and attempted to hand it to Gregory.

"You must place this behind the Snagon's ear and press the amber light. It will die instantly and feel no pain. We will do the rest Fire Head," she said in a reassuring tone.

"I'm not going to do that," Gregory protested, pushing the device away. "The Snagon is out cold! It is not harming anyone, so why do we have to kill it? I will defend myself if I am being attacked, but I won't kill an animal while it sleeps. I think *that* is cowardly!"

"We are not heartless," said Placid. "The beast must die for it is controlled by Mediana the Sorceress. If you do not kill it, the creature may come back to harm us in the future. Do you want that on your conscience?"

"No," Gregory said, taking the gadget off the captain. He reluctantly walked over to the Snagon, placing the weapon behind its right ear. Gregory hesitated.

"Do it now before it wakes up," ordered Placid impatiently.

He was about to press the amber light, when he remembered what Mezra said about acting with kindness. The Snagon stirred and opened its eyes. It seemed petrified, as if it knew what was about to happen, and started to whimper. One of the figures laughed, "look at you now, foolish Snagon. Your time is over."

Gregory spoke softly in the Snagon's ear, "I do not want to kill you, so fly away and don't come back". The creature rose and flapped its mighty wings, and in one swift movement flew off at blistering speed.

"Why did you let it go?" roared the private. "You may have cost countless lives!"

"It does not matter now Private; we need to leave this place at once. Climb on board Fire Head," said Captain Placid, as two of the figures held a piece of cloth between them making a seat.

"My name is not Fire Head, it is Gregory!"
He jumped up and sat on the cloth as they set off rapidly across the Spongey Lake. It felt as though he were sitting on a swing.

"Where are we going?" he asked. No one answered and Gregory did not repeat the question; he just held on and enjoyed the ride. They were travelling extremely fast, but strangely he could not feel any wind against his face. They passed many peculiar landscapes that were all uniquely beautiful, and Gregory was in awe.

After a while they came to a jagged mountain. The group headed towards it and entered a dark cave at its base. When they got inside Gregory was surprised to see that they were in a spectacular mountain city. He was taken into a curious stone building without a roof.

"You may come down now," said Placid. He hastily got down off the cloth and stretched his legs.

"Allow me to formally introduce myself. I am Captain Placid, leader of the Mellow Patrol. Welcome to the mountain stronghold."

Placid was a giant figure and Gregory strained his neck to look up at her. She had pale yellow skin and three legs.

"I am Gregory Butler. Glad to meet you." He was feeling tired and a little worse for wear because of the knock to his head. Gregory gave a wide yawn. "Sorry," he said covering his mouth. The events of the day were catching up with him.

"You should get some rest now and we will talk later," said Placid kindly. "There is so much you need to know about and so little time."

She turned to one of the other creatures, "Private Tranquil, show Gregory to his rest zone."

"Yes, Captain," said Private Tranquil, and led Gregory to his sleeping chamber. It was an immaculately clean, small, white room. The only objects there were an oval shaped bed, side table, and a chair.

"Could I get something to eat, please?" asked Gregory. The snacks in his backpack would soon be completely gone. He thought about the meal he had eaten earlier, and it seemed days ago.

"No problem, make yourself comfortable and I will have some food brought to you," said Tranquil, as she hovered out of the room. Gregory sat down on the bed and removed his trainers. *I will just rest for a while until the food comes,* he thought, as he lay back and nestled into the soft bed, drifting off to sleep.

While he was sleeping, news spread around the mountain city that a strange boy had escaped a Snagon and dropped from the sky. Everybody wanted to see him because the prophets had foretold that a Fire Head would lead them back to the Kingdom of Mellow.

They were badgering Captain Placid to wake the visitor up so they could meet him, but she insisted that they wait until Gregory finished resting. However, one young Mellow girl was too excited to wait and had convinced her mother, Private Tranquil, to allow her to take him some food. She hurriedly made her way to the rest zone and entered the chamber.

"I knew you would come," she said excitedly.

Gregory woke up as soon as he heard her voice. He sat up on the bed and looked across the chamber. There he saw the most beautiful girl that he had ever seen in his life. She was not like the others that brought him to the mountain. The girl was the same height as him and had two legs. She was not floating over the ground but walking towards him with a meal.

"What did you say?"

"I am sorry… I thought you were awake," said the girl nervously. "Here, this is for you." She held out the container and inside was a green ball about the size of a large apple, but it had rough skin like an orange.

"What is it?"

 Gregory took the strange item from her and toyed with it in his fingers. "Is it a ball?" He asked, throwing it in the air.

The girl looked at him, bemused. 'It's a sap-sop," she said. "Don't you have them where you are from?"

He inspected it closely and sniffed the skin. "I am not sure! I don't think so. If we do, I have never seen them. What does it taste like?" asked, Gregory, keen to know more before he tried it.

"Whatever you like. They are extraordinarily delicious," she said, with a disarming smile.

He took a bite and began to chew slowly. "It has no taste," said Gregory, disappointedly.

"No, it definitely has a taste. Maybe you do not understand: it is 'thinking food.' Whatever you want it to taste like, that's the flavour it will have. Just think of a flavour," said the girl.

Once again, he bit the sap-sop, but this time he thought about Chinese food. It tasted lovely, exactly like the food at the restaurant. After that he took another bite and thought of vanilla ice cream. The taste was so good he took two more bites of vanilla ice cream from the sap-sop. Then to wash it all down, Gregory imagined he was drinking freshly squeezed pineapple juice. He felt the pineapple nectar run down the back of his throat.

"That was incredible!" said Gregory in amazement. "What is it called again?"

Their conversation felt very comfortable. Which was strange because at home he never spoke to girls as he was too shy.

"A sap-sop," she said, smiling. "We have many sap-sop trees here in the stronghold." Gregory forgot about being tired.

"I heard that you escaped from a Snagon at the Spongey Lake. Is it true?" she asked.

"Yes, I did," he said, puffing out his chest, feeling rather pleased with himself. He was liking this 'hero business' more and more, as he had never got so much attention before.

"Then you must be here to help us. We have been waiting a long time for you to come. My mother told me about the prophecy, but I never thought that I would get to meet you in person."

"Err… well, yes I am." Gregory wasn't sure what to say. "I'm not trying to be rude, but how come you are not like those other people?" he asked, but as soon as he finished the question, he felt embarrassed. *She will know that I am interested in her,* he thought.

"What do you mean? We are all people of Mellow," she said, clearly puzzled by his question.

He was not sure whether to pursue the topic or not. After all, he was here to complete a task. "Well, for a start, you don't have three legs. The other Mellows that brought me here did.

Also, you are normal size, but Captain Placid and the rest of the patrol are enormous."

She started to giggle, "Oh. you are so silly; all the Mellow Patrol are thirds. I am not. Don't you have thirds in your land?"

The girl took a seat next to him on the bed.

"What is a third?" Gregory did not want to sound foolish, but he had no idea what she was talking about.

"Our people only have children once in a lifetime. They always have three at a time and one of them has three legs. That is why they are called thirds; because they have a third leg."

"Oh, I see!" Gregory said. But he didn't really understand what she meant; he was just being polite.

"What about their height? Why are they so tall?"

The girl got up off the bed and walked towards the door with the empty food container in her hand.

"That is just how they are," she said defensively.

Placid entered the room and she did not look happy with the fact Gregory had company. The girl was startled and dropped the empty container on the floor.

"Win, what are you doing here?" Placid asked with an intimidating glare as she towered over her.

"I came to bring a sap-sop." Win answered nervously, her head bowed. She hurriedly picked up the container off the floor and stood back up, trembling.

"You know that you should not be here. Leave us at once!" said Placid firmly. Win apologised to the captain, then said a quick goodbye to Gregory before leaving hastily.

"Gregory, we are glad you are here with us. I have called a meeting of the Mellow Council and they would like you to attend. The meeting will take place in a few hours, so get some rest and we will talk again later. This time I will ensure that you are not interrupted." Placid still looked quite angry.

"Okay, Captain Placid. Please don't be too hard on Win. We were only talking about my task here."

Placid turned her back to him and hovered out of the chamber. Gregory rested his head down on the bed, but this time did not fall asleep so easily.

Meanwhile, over on the Spongey Lake, Skrimp and the Special Guard were hunting for him. They had located the spot where he fell from the sky, and Luda the tracker was searching the ground for clues. Luda was a specialist and soon picked up his footprints. After a few metres the tracks ended.

"What's wrong? Why have you stopped?" asked Skrimp. She was an impatient leader who pressured those in her command constantly. To be a member of the Special Guard was not easy.

"The trail has gone dead! Something happened here," Luda said. She wiped the sweat off her brow and began to sniff the air. "I am not sure what took place, but it was within the last few hours."

"What are you talking about Luda?" Skrimp was agitated. "In the last few hours means nothing to me. Try and pick it up again."

Luda inhaled deeply, "There is a faint smell coming from that direction." She gestured towards the large set of red mountains across the lake.

"Let's go," ordered Skrimp.

They all set off towards the mountains. When they got to the edge of the Spongey Lake there were two huge indentations in the ground.

"Two giant creatures fell here," said Luda, sniffing one of the hollows. "The scent of the intruder is overpowering, but there is no trail. It does not make sense." She looked around in bewilderment, searching for an answer that would satisfy Skrimp.

"That's not good enough, we need to find him immediately. King Berserk does not accept failure." Skrimp was pacing up and down. It would only be a matter of seconds before Luda felt the tip of her arrow.

She ran over to the other indentation and sniffed. "This imprint was made by a Snagon," she said, knowing that this information would save her life.

"A Snagon? Are you sure?" asked Skrimp. This was the breakthrough that she needed, as to return to Berserk empty handed was a mistake that the band of torment would not let you repeat twice. "Yes, definitely a Snagon," Luda said.

Skrimp smiled for the first time since they had left the palace. "Let us go and find Mediana."

THE MOUNTAIN CITY

The Mellow Council meeting was in session, and the twenty-four elders of the executive were seated around a large semi-circular table. It took place in the main hall which was a cavern chiselled out of the mountain interior. They were already deep in discussion when Placid entered the conference with Gregory. The chamber went silent as they both stood before the council.

Captain Placid was invited to speak and stood up behind the podium. "Thank you for attending this meeting. I am pleased to introduce Gregory Butler, the Fire Head foretold of in our prophecy. We will now formulate our plan to return our people to the Kingdom of Mellow."

"Greetings, Placid, it is a good day. We have received a message from King Cordial, and he is aware of Fire Head's presence. He warned us that Berserk has sent the Special Guard to find him, so time is of the essence. We must make haste," said the chief elder.

Gregory gulped in shock at the news that he was being hunted. The elder continued, "King Cordial has commanded that we approach King Griscat and ask him for help in this matter."

"King Griscat will not help us. He is too proud to break his agreement with Queen Flora. I am not sure we will be able to persuade him," said one of the council members.

"Perhaps he will think differently now that the Fire Head is here," said Placid.

"We are not here to question King Cordial, but to obey his commands," asserted the chief elder. "The ambassador has already been sent to seek King Griscat's assistance."

Gregory was surprised by how young the elder looked. She had a normal sized body and the same long, dark hair as the other Mellow women. Her nose was fleshy and a bit yellower than the rest of her face.

"Yes, Councillor," Placid answered, and bowed her head. "Please allow me to take Fire Head to the Garden of Fruitful Knowledge, to bring him up to date with the situation," she humbly asked. "Under the circumstances it is important that he is brought up to speed as soon as mellowly possible."

"It is forbidden, as you are aware Captain Placid. No outsider can enter the garden. It is only for the people of Mellow. A foreigner has never stepped foot in our sacred place," the elder reminded her firmly.

"This is a special situation. He must enter to fully understand his role. The Fire Head is here to help free us, so how can we class him as an outsider?" said Placid.

"You make a compelling argument," said the elder. "We shall confer on the matter. Leave us." The elder began to speak to the other council members. They were all talking over each other, and Gregory wondered how they could even hear themselves.

Placid turned to Gregory, "Follow me," she said, and led him out of the hall. They went into the corridor and sat on a large bench. The captain told him all about the war between the people of Mellow and the people of Rage. King Berserk had used deceit and witchcraft to defeat the people of Mellow and take over their kingdom to satisfy his greed.

"So, the Kingdom of Rage is really your land?" Gregory asked. He had yet to meet Berserk but already had a dislike for him. "Berserk sounds like a nasty piece of work. He reminds me of someone I know back home."

"Yes, the Mellow people lived peacefully for more than five thousand years. It used to be known as the land of light - an idyllic place before Berserk turned it into complete chaos," Placid said sadly.

At that moment, a messenger came to call them back into the main hall. Placid and Gregory stood before the executive council of elders once again.

"We have decided to allow Fire Head to enter the garden," said the elder.

Placid turned to Gregory, "I hope you realise that this is a great privilege. We are trusting you to keep any information you learn to yourself."

"I will," he said confidently.

Placid bowed towards the council and left with Gregory, heading for the garden. They walked silently along the corridor and then through a narrower passageway to an open space. Placid and Gregory crossed a golden bridge and entered a large, beautiful orchard. "*Wow!*" Gregory gasped in awe, breaking the silence. All the trees were multi-coloured and bore strange shaped fruits. There were many sap-sop trees amongst them with ripe green fruits hanging temptingly from their branches. This is the Garden of Fruitful Knowledge," Placid informed him. "All that we know comes from these trees."

Gregory was admiring the variety of fruits. "This is a very beautiful place," he said, inhaling the pleasant cocktail of fruit in the air. The captain led him along a path until they came to a small tree. The bark was dark grey, and it had shiny red crystal-like berries that were surrounded by clusters of blue leaves.

"These are the prophets," she said, plucking some of the berries with her long fingers. "Their knowledge has been passed down from generation to generation. They have been our source of hope during these trials with Berserk."

"I don't understand what you mean," said a rather puzzled Gregory. He was straining his neck to look up at Placid.

"The berries of prophecy are our fruit of the future. They guide us along life's journey," said Placid, with a warm smile. "When you eat them, you are shown what is to come. They are the ones that told us you will help take back the land of Mellow."

"Really?' asked Gregory. 'What about all the other trees around here? What do they do?"

"Let me show you," Placid led him over to the biggest tree in the orchard. It was thick with red bark and had many branches. Each branch was covered in yellow buds. "This is the Tree of Past Times. All that has gone before can be seen by using the buds of this tree," said Placid, who was now glowing with enthusiasm. She told Gregory to pick some and put them in his pocket.

"They are very high up. Could you take some for me?" asked Gregory.

She explained that the berries should be hand-picked by him and no one else. The fruit only showed things relevant to those who chose them. So, he stretched up on tiptoes and picked some.

He looked around and saw that other Mellows were entering the orchard and began to feel nervous as they stared at him. Placid recognised his discomfort. "Don't be afraid. They are just curious," she said, reassuringly looking down at him. He smiled uneasily.

Placid led him further into the garden, "This is the Tree of Death," she pointed towards a sickly-looking tree. It was transparent with small white leaves. "If you were to eat from this one, within a very short time you would become old and die."

"That sounds horrible! Why do you keep a tree like that?" Gregory asked. As a toddler he used to put everything in his mouth and shuddered at the thought that someone could eat it by mistake.

Captain Placid stared at the tree. "At one time there were many Mellows who could not see the point of keeping a tree that causes harm. They wanted us to destroy it and never let it grow again."

"What happened?" Gregory asked.

"King Cordial decided that the tree should remain. He said that it had always been with our people, so must have a purpose of benefit to the Mellows."

Placid turned from the tree and looked at him. "As usual, the King was proven right. Shortly after his decision, the kingdom was infested by disgusting creatures called Grataz. They brought with them a deadly plague, and many Mellows died. We had no choice but to use the tree of death to eradicate them. We crushed the leaves and spread it onto their favourite food. The Grataz were killed and the Kingdom of Mellow cleansed."

The number of Mellows in the garden had quickly increased from a handful to over a hundred. "Come," Placid said, as she held out her open hand. Gregory took hold of it and felt even more nervous, as her hand was three times the size of his.

She led him to the other side of the orchard where they came to a long, thin tree. The tree had metallic blue bark that glimmered in the light. It did not go straight up, but zig-zagged its way from the bottom to the top. On the end of every green branch were five brown nuts.

"Try one of these," instructed Placid, as she stretched out her long arms and took down a couple of nuts

"What are they?" Gregory asked, apprehensively.

"Try it and find out. Just take off the skin." Gregory took a nut and stood still. He looked around and there were even more Mellows. Gregory felt very uncomfortable and disliked them all watching him.

"Do not be afraid. The people of Mellow are overjoyed by the news that you have come. This is the long-awaited day. They know that your arrival is a sign that our misery will soon be over. Every Mellow has been praying to leave this mountain and return to our own kingdom."

Gregory peeled off the nutshell and took a bite. He began to chew for a few seconds and then stopped. A warm feeling of pure joy overtook him, and he started to laugh. Placid and all the Mellows standing around him joined in, and the garden became a symphony of laughter. He was at one with the people of Mellow even though he had only just met them.

"You see, Fire Head. The nut of joy will erase your concerns."

Meanwhile, Skrimp and the Special Guard were on their way to visit Mediana in her lair. She dwelt in the Valley of Kwingo, underneath the volcano. The Special Guard were infamous throughout the kingdom for their cruel actions. As well as Skrimp and her deadly Droll, there was: Yallon the Mighty, Merew the Torturer, Porma the Pulveriser, Blink-Speed, Luda the Tracker and Comron the Claw.

When the Special Guard were near the valley, they were ambushed by a group of hungry, giant piranha-teeth wolves. These were fearsome creatures with a taste for flesh. The wolves had eight long legs that were covered in sharp points. Their bodies had silver scales which they could use to temporarily blind their prey. But their most deadly weapon was their venomous, razor-like piranha-teeth. They lived a feral life in the wastelands, and always hunted in packs.

Skrimp opened fire with the arrows from her Droll, and Yallon began to expertly wield his sword, slashing several wolves to pieces. Porma was pulverising them with her Itey (a type of heavy mallet). Luda and the rest were hiding behind the giant frame of Comron, who was ripping the piranha-teeth apart with his claws.

When all the piranha-teeth were killed, the Special Guard looked around at each other. "That was fun," said Skrimp. "Too easy!" Comron responded, "Are there anymore?"

Skrimp signalled that they should continue their journey. The huge Kwingo volcano was bubbling noisily above them as they entered the valley. They walked a while and came to the entrance to Mediana's lair. It was hidden behind a flowing waterfall that rained down from high, producing a torrent of steamy water. All the Special Guard were silent as they cautiously made their way up the steep, slippery rocks.

Comron lagged well behind the rest of the guard, awkwardly manoeuvring his large frame between the rocks. Blink-Speed began to mock him, "come on big lump! Get that fat backside moving." Her super speed made him look even more slow and cumbersome than he was.

"I will crush you!" Comron shouted in frustration. He was not someone to be messed with and had no sense of humour.

"The only thing you will crush are the rocks," she said, laughing. Blink-speed was darting up and down, tormenting him. The rest of the guard continued, ignoring their antics. Blink-Speed provoked him further by waving her hands in his face while just out of reach.

"Why, you little flea!" Comron yelled and swung his big arm, clumsily trying to hit her; but he was too slow. The momentum made him lose balance and he fell from a great height into the rock pool underneath the waterfall. He landed awkwardly on his back and screamed out in pain. Blink-Speed was down at his side in an instant. She cradled his head in her arms and looked up to the rest of the group.

"What are you doing?" asked Skrimp, staring down into the pool.

"We need to help him." Blink-Speed shouted up in desperation, realising that her foolishness had caused this terrible situation.

"We do not have time," Skrimp replied.

"We cannot just leave him!" Blink-Speed roared in outrage, just before an arrow entered Comron's large chest. Skrimp lowered her Drad and turned to enter the cave behind the waterfall.

The remaining Special Guard members silently followed her. Blink-Speed sat rocking back and forth with Comron's head in her lap for a few seconds, before joining them.

Back at the castle, King Berserk was in his sleeping chamber tossing and turning in the bed. "No, no, no," he whimpered. He sounded tormented as he wrestled with the demons in his mind. "NO!" King Berserk howled loudly, and one of his guards ran in to the room to wake him up.

"Are you alright Your Majesty?" he asked, shaking the King's shoulder. Beserk immediately ceased howling and opened his eyes. He sat up, the band of torment began to glow red. The guard started to scream and ran towards the door, holding his head while shrieking in pain. His body levitated high until it almost touched the ceiling before it was thrown back to the ground. Another guard ran in and looked down on the floor, horrified to see his friend's lifeless body.

"Take him away." Berserk fumed. The veins on the side of his thick neck were protruding, and he had a crazed look in his eyes. He was sitting in the bed looking like he had risen from an eerie grave.

"Yes, my Lord." The guard called for assistance with removing the body.

Berserk got up off the bed and put on his royal robe. He exited the room onto the balcony and went to rest his arms on the wall overlooking the courtyard. As he stared out into the night sky, gazing up at the myriad of stars, he called out softly. "Flora, I need you. Why have you abandoned me?" He looked to the left and the right, as if searching for his dead wife.

"Why have you gone away?" King Berserk cried out desperately into the night. Then he put both hands on his head, bent down and cried. "Come back…" he said softly.

His moment of self-pity was broken by a noise coming from below. He looked down in the courtyard. It was dark and he could hardly make out several figures around the guard post.

"Who is that?" he shouted into the darkness.

"It is me, my Lord, your servant Latip."

"What are you doing?" the King demanded angrily.

Berserk had never liked Latip, and would have surely killed him long ago, but he had a grudging sense of gratitude because Latip had helped Queen Flora when she first came to the kingdom. The Queen had become very sick, and it was the herbs that Latip found for her that had cured her disease.

"I am making arrangements for the return of the magra service," said Latip hastily.

"So be it!" Berserk grunted and walked to the other side of the balcony. He stood still and looked up at the four crescent moons in the night sky, and their pale-yellow light illuminated the contours of his savage face.

THE CHALLENGE

Gregory sat relaxing in the rest zone. On the table beside him was a plate with some buds from the Tree of Past Times, along with a few red crystal berries of prophecy.

He was ready to discover the truth; so, Gregory took two of the yellow buds off the plate, put them in his mouth, and laid his head down on the pillow. As soon as he closed his eyes, a vision appeared. He saw the picturesque land of Mellow flowing with love and light. It was full of laughing people who were living happily. There were old and young Mellows singing and dancing in the courtyard of the palace before the King and Queen.

A dark shadow came over them as a Snagon swooped down and took the Queen away. Then everyone began to flee as Berserk's army attacked.

Gregory shuddered on the bed as horrendous images flashed through his mind of battles, blood, death, and destruction. His eyes opened when the images became too much for him to endure.

The grotesque face of Berserk sitting on the Mellow throne laughing at the carnage, imprinted itself in his mind.

Gregory paced up and down, contemplating what he had witnessed. *I need to see the future now.* He sat back down on the bed and reached for the berries of prophecy, but paused when he heard a small voice crying for help.

At first, he thought that it was a figment of his imagination. However, he soon realised that the voice was coming from inside his sleeping zone. "Where are you?" Gregory tentatively asked.

"I am down here. You'd better let me out! I can't take it much longer," the muffled voice said, very annoyed.

"Where are you?" Gregory asked, quite sure he was going mad.

"I am trapped under this rock," the voice replied. Gregory started to walk to the end of the bed, and it grew louder. "Get me out!"

"There are no rocks in here!" Gregory said, confused at what he was hearing, "but if you keep talking, I will try to find you." He got down on all fours and looked around the room. There were no rocks there, only his backpack. "Where are you? Stop playing games!" He was beginning to lose patience.

Then Gregory saw it - a small, bushy tail sticking out from under the backpack. "Now I can see you. I am going to get you out if you promise to be calm."

"I promise," the creature said meekly.

He carefully lifted the backpack, and a furry animal ran straight at him and bit him on the toe. He held his foot, with the creature still attached to it, and started hopping up and down in pain. After a few seconds, the animal let go.

"What the heck is wrong with you?" Gregory said still holding his foot. "Why would you bite someone who was helping you? I could have left you trapped under there if I wanted to."

"Helping me! You're the one who trapped me," said the furry animal indignantly.

"Hold on a minute!" Gregory interrupted. 'I did no such thing. That is not a trap, it is just my backpack. Why would I trap you? I love animals. What are you talking about?"

"Yes, you did. You put that sweet-smelling food inside the rock and how could Wedger resist that? When I went to eat it, your trap set, and I have been stuck under there for hours." Gregory looked closely at Wedger. He was orangey-brown and had a bushy tail. Wedger had chocolate smeared around his claws and mouth. "Oh, I see, you like chocolate," said Gregory with a smile. "It's also one of my favourite snacks."

He picked up the backpack and showed it to Wedger. "This is not a trap. It's just where I keep important things." Gregory opened it and poured out the contents onto the bed.

"Let's start again," he said, taking out the only remaining chocolate bar. He broke off a piece and gave it to his new furry friend. Wedger snatched it from his hand and promptly stuffed it in his mouth.

"'My name is Gregory."

Wedger was busy munching away at the chocolate. "Don't think you can bribe me with gifts. I have great honour and high standards." Wedger belched loudly, and then continued to munch furiously.

"You don't have to eat so fast Wedger. That will give you indigestion. Take your time."

Wedger ate the rest of the chocolate, scanning the contents on the bed at the same time. "Is that more chocolate?" he asked, gulping down the last piece.

"What, this?" Gregory removed his harmonica from its case and cleaned it with a cloth. He kept it in excellent condition, and it was almost as good as new. "No, it is my harmonica."

"Harmonica? What is that? Does it taste good?" Wedger was eager to eat it. His species could eat ten times their own body weight in one sitting.

"It is not for eating; it is for music," said Gregory. "I almost forgot that I had it in there. I could play you a tune if you like."

"What's a tune?" Wedger asked, slightly disappointed that he could not eat.

Gregory put the instrument to his mouth and began to play. It was a lively song that his father had taught him. Wedger was mesmerised and stood on top of the bed doing a silly dance. Jumping and swaying, spinning, and twirling, laughing, and even doing summersaults at one point.

When the tune finished playing, Wedger collapsed and lay on his back with his arms wide open. "That was fun," he said tiredly.

"Yes, it was," said Gregory, also resting on the bed.

Suddenly, there was a scream followed by a crashing noise, and they both quickly sat up. Win was standing at the door with a look of horror on her face. She had dropped a tray of sap-sop on the floor, several of which had rolled under the table.

"Get it off the bed!" she shouted hysterically.

"No, it's alright. Wedger is my friend," he said, trying to calm her down.

"Get it out of here!" she shouted again, looking absolutely horrified.

Wedger turned to Gregory. "What is wrong with her? She is ruining the party." Then he settled back onto the bed looking quite relaxed.

"It's okay, Wedger, I think she is just shocked." Gregory got up and picked the tray and sap-sop off the floor, placing them on the bed. Wedger dived onto the sap-sop and started to chomp away.

"Wow, don't you ever stop eating? You are like a machine," said Gregory.

Win was watching their interaction open mouthed. "How can you talk to animals? Where did you learn to do that?" she enquired.

"I just can," said Gregory.

"You can understand what this noisy person is saying, and speak her language. How do you do that?" Wedger asked, wiping away the sap-sop juice trickling down his chin.

"I just can." Gregory repeated, as he gathered his things off the bed and returned them to his backpack.

Over in the land off the Feliroo, the Mellow ambassador and three thirds were approaching the outer walls of Catabong Palace. Two of the thirds were carrying the ambassador on a cloth seat, like the one they had carried Gregory on. The other third was on lookout duty. A guard of fifty Feliroo rushed out and approached them.

"Stop here," the ambassador ordered. The Mellows came to a halt. When the Feliroo guards were close to the ambassador, they made a straight formation. Their javelins were sharp and glistening as they sized up the Mellows.

A voice cried out, "I am Themdar of the Feliroo. State your business here!"

Themdar was known throughout all the kingdoms as a warrior of valour.

"I am the Mellow ambassador. We are here in peace, Themdar. I have come to seek an audience with King Griscat," she said in the Feliroo language.

"Follow me," Themdar said, and the Feliroo guards led the Mellows into the palace. Once inside the palace gates Themdar made them wait in the outer courtyard. They were surrounded by Feliroo soldiers training for combat. Their fighting skills were second to none. They were fast and lethally accurate with their weapons.

After a short while, the ambassador was called into the throne room. King Griscat sat majestically on the golden throne of Geba. He beckoned the Mellow ambassador over and she went before him and bowed.

"State your business," said the King authoritatively.

"Your Majesty, we are here to request your help in our fight against Berserk," said the ambassador.

King Griscat shook his head in disapproval. "I have made my position on that matter clear. I will not wage war on King Berserk. We have a peace agreement."

"With all respect Your Majesty. Berserk is a tyrant, and it is only a matter of time before he invades your land, just as he invaded the Kingdom of Mellow," the ambassador pleaded.

"Now is the time to overthrow him before he becomes too strong."

'You are aware that a Feliroo does not break an agreement. Our word is our bond. If King Berserk is foolish enough to attack us, we will show him why Feliroo warriors are revered across the kingdoms."

"The Fire Head is here Your Majesty. This is the season when the prophecy will come to pass. We must unite and overthrow the evil one," pressed the ambassador.

"I do not believe in your prophecy. It is superstitious nonsense," said King Griscat dismissively.

"Berserk is using dark forces. He is preparing to raise an army from the grave to destroy this world. Even your mighty soldiers are no match for such a force," the ambassador continued.

"Silence, you bore me with your idle tales. Refresh yourself and rest, then make your way back to your people," said the King.

"Yes, Your Majesty," the ambassador replied disappointedly. Once the ambassador had left the room, the King's son approached the throne.

"Father, we must go and fight alongside the Mellows."

"My son, it is not the way of our people to break a treaty."

"A treaty with the devil is not one that should be kept. We are a people of courage. Let us not sit idly by and watch an oppressor terrorise our lands," said the prince.

"You are young and foolish my son. The Feliroo are a people of integrity and do not break oaths."

"We are not cowards Father. Those people have already broken the treaty by crossing the border to steal our Akiti and we do nothing. Where is the integrity in *that*?" the prince asked rebelliously.

"Leave me. I will hear no more of this," said the King sternly. The prince stormed out of the throne room and into the inner palace. Themdar the warrior was waiting for him. "Prince Droll, you should not approach the King in that way," she chastised.

"Themdar, you are a warrior. Can you not convince him to fight against Berserk? You can see that war is the only answer."

"The King has many counsellors, and I am one of his protectors. I will speak to him when his temper has subdued." Themdar stated.

At the same time, over in the Valley of Kwingo, the Special Guard were seated around a dirty sandstone table in Mediana's lair. Skrimp was at the head. Yallon was sitting nearest to her, playing with his sword. Porma was at the middle of the table, drinking ale from a giant tankard with Luda and Merew. Blink-Speed was sitting quietly at the other end by herself.

Luda arose and sat next to Blink-Speed. "Shake it off, soldier," she said, placing her hand tenderly on Blink-Speed's arm, who lowered her head again and stared blankly at the table still in shock over Comron's death.

Mediana appeared in their midst. "Have you all rested?" she asked in her slippery voice.

"We have wasted enough time resting, Mediana," scorned Skrimp, "Where is the Fire Head?"

"He is with the Feliroo in the Kingdom of Geba."

"How can this be?" Skrimp asked in surprise. "That would be an act of war. King Griscat would not break the peace treaty to protect an outsider."

Mediana waved her hand over the floor in a circular motion, "let me show you." Smoke rose from the ground and, as it cleared, they had an aerial view of Droll and Yord standing by the large hole. The image suddenly froze and then turned blank.

"What is happening now?" Skrimp demanded to know.

"Wait," said Mediana, "the Snagon stream will come back on. I think that the Fire Head attacked it with some type of weapon and knocked it out of the sky."

After a short while, the images spluttered and reappeared with the Snagon waking up on the floor looking at Gregory. Then the terrified beast escaped by flying off into the sky. The images did not show the Mellow Patrol.

"Now I understand why King Berserk said that I should not go alone to kill him. Fire Head has powers," said Skrimp.

"He also has formidable allies in the Feliroo," Luda added.

"Have you contacted King Berserk and told him what has happened?" Skrimp asked Mediana.

"Not yet. I am meeting with him shortly."

'Okay, you inform him of the situation, and we will make our way back to the palace to prepare for war," said Skimp. The Special Guard rose from their seats and followed her out.

Mediana teleported her hologram to the Gantmas' burial ground, at the foot of the red mountains of Tevro.

The Gantmas were an ancient warrior people that became extinct during the great deluge. Their whole kingdom was flooded under water for three hundred years.

According to legend, their traditions were steeped in occult practices and their warlocks could manifest powerful spells. The Gantmas were said to have owned a sinister magic wand called the Nactu, with which the dead could be raised and controlled.

When Mediana's hologram appeared at the burial site, many unfortunate creatures were digging and sifting through material. They were all dressed in the recognisable grey tunics of King Berserk's slaves. As soon as they realised that Mediana was there, they downed their tools and stopped working.

A large creature with the body of an ape and head of a boar was in charge. He walked towards Mediana and bowed.

"Ret, what have you found?" Mediana asked, ringing her hands.

"We have found nothing." He pointed to the mountain face. "I am sure the Nactu is on the other side of the Tevro. That is Feliroo land, and we cannot dig there."

"Berserk will not be pleased," Mediana warned. As she turned the palms of her hands to face the sky, all the slaves started to run as fast as their legs would carry them. Five of the workers began writhing in pain and keeled over.

"Find the Nactu," she said, as they lay dying in agony on the floor. Then her hologram faded away.

Meanwhile, over in the stench and squalor of King Berserk's dungeon, Latip was once again in conversation with King Cordial. They were sitting opposite each other at the table.

"Your Majesty, there is good news regarding the Fire Head. He is currently under the protection of the Mellow Patrol in the mountain city." Latip poured out some water for the King.

"That is splendid news Latip. What is the situation with King Griscat?" he enquired as he took a thirsty gulp from the goblet.

"The ambassador was sent as you ordered, Your Majesty. She should return today with an answer."

King Cordial was happy. "What of the magra ceremony? Have you put everything in place?"

"Oh yes, everything is going to plan with the event. It will be a celebration that will be remembered for a long time, my Lord," he said mischievously.

"A toast, to a bright and prosperous future, my friend," said the King. And they both raised their goblets to the Kingdom of Mellow.

THE PREPARATION

Gregory spent his time in the mountain city learning about the history of the Mellows and the ancient prophecies. Everyone was eagerly waiting for the ambassador to return with a response from King Griscat.

Captain Placid took him along to the Mellow training camp. They were perfecting their techniques in preparation for battle.

"You must equip yourself for what is to come," she informed him. There were many types of weapons in the camp: swords; axes; staffs; and a lethal discus weapon called a Nid. The Nid was very popular amongst the troops as it returned to the thrower like a boomerang.

Gregory wanted to test out the weapons to see which one would suit him. First, he tried to pick up a sword. It was so heavy that when he attempted to lift it, he fell over backwards onto the floor. Some of the troops laughed as he struggled to get up. Then a little head popped out of his trouser pocket.

"Do you want me to call a medic?" It was Wedger.

"What the heck, Wedger. Have you been in there all the time?" Gregory asked. "I do not need you poking fun today."

Wedger climbed up onto his shoulder and sat down. "Stop feeling sorry for yourself, Fire Head. Aren't you the hero who has come to free the land?"

Gregory thought for a moment, "Yes, I am." He tried to lift the sword again, but he could not.

"Try something else, Fire Head," said Wedger. "A Nid, maybe!"

Gregory picked up a Nid and threw it, but the discus landed only a couple of metres away from him. "It is no use. These weapons are not for me," he said, feeling defeated.

"How did you get this far?" Wedger asked.

"My glasses got me here," Gregory pointed to his specs.

"What are glasses?" asked Wedger in puzzlement.

"These things I am wearing on my eyes." Gregory took the glasses off.

"Wow. I thought they were part of your face," Wedger said. "Put them back on, you are one ugly Fire Head," he joked.

"Thanks, Wedger," he replied, sarcastically.

"What do they do for you?" Wedger asked, curiously.

"I only know what a few of the settings do. I will show you." He put the glasses back on, pressed down the button on the side and became invisible. Everyone around him gasped as it seemed that Wedger was floating in mid-air.

Then Gregory clicked the switch up and became visible. "Can you do anything else, Fire Head?"

"Sure, I can," he replied, growing in confidence. He picked up Wedger from his shoulder and placed him on the floor. Then he turned the setting on his glasses to number two and started to shrink. Slowly he decreased in size until they were roughly the same height, looking at each other eyeball to eyeball on the floor.

Wedger started talking to Gregory, but he did not understand him because his glasses were not on the right setting. Gregory turned the dial to number one and grew back to normal. He looked down at tiny Wedger who was still squeaking incoherently.

"You sound better like this," Gregory said, chuckling as he turned the dial setting to number three so he could understand his friend again.

Wedger ran back up Gregory's body and repositioned himself on his shoulder.

"That is incredible. Can you do more? Can you fly? Or jump higher than a mountain? Or fire lasers from your eyes? Can you? Can you?" He was extremely excited, his bushy tail thrashing back and forth.

"Calm down, little fellow. I can turn myself into a giant, but I am still learning what my powers are."

"Well, how many powers do you have? Do you know?"

"I have twelve powers, but I only know four so far. Universal language, invisibility, shrinking, and becoming a giant. I just need to discover the others."

"What are you waiting for?" Wedger held up his fists and started shadow boxing. "We are going to beat them senseless."

Gregory laughed. "I will try and find out what my other powers are, but only if you go and sit far away. I don't want you to get hurt," he said, pointing into the distance.

"I am a Wedger of action, almost indestructible, and danger is my middle name."

"Seriously, go and sit over there. I mean it."

"Okay," Wedger acquiesced reluctantly, running down Gregory's arm and moving far away.

Gregory turned the dial setting to number four. He waited a few seconds, and nothing happened.

"What is going on?' shouted Wedger. "Let's get the party started already. I ain't got all day." Wedger waited a few more seconds. "I am falling asleep here, Fire Head. What are you gonna do? Bore Berserks army to death?" He was now rolling on the floor laughing.

It was time to try another setting, so Gregory turned the dial to number five. He waited a little while and still nothing happened. Wedger was still chuckling in the distance. Gregory looked over and could see a stray Nid flying in his direction.

"Look out!" he cried to his friend, but Wedger was still busy laughing, oblivious to the danger. Gregory dashed towards him, and, in a fraction of a second, he caught the Nid with his hand just before it hit Wedger.

Wedger gulped as the Nid was a hair's width from his face. "You saved my life, Fire Head." Tears welled in his eyes, "You are a true pal!"

"Don't mention it, my friend," Gregory smiled at him. "Now we can also add super speed to my powers."

Wedger looked a bit shook up and started to back away. "You know what? That was a close call. I will see you later," he said as he scampered off into the distance.

Gregory went back to training. He now knew that setting five was super speed, and wanted to discover more powers. So, he tried setting six on his glasses and nothing happened. Next, setting seven; and still no joy. He was just about to try number eight, when a voice called out his name. It was Win, and she was smiling at him.

"Hi, Gregory, how is the training?"

"It's getting a bit frustrating, to be honest".

"Do you want to see something interesting?" she asked.

"Yes, I would," he replied.

Win looked over to Captain Placid. "Can I take Gregory to see Azucar Rocks?" she asked.

"I don't think that is wise." Placid answered.

"We will stay within the mountain city," she pleaded.

"I would like to see it," Gregory chipped in.

"Okay," said Placid. "Do not be too long, stay within the city, and return to base in one hour."

Win and Gregory made their way out of the training camp. They walked along the shiny path and spoke about the Mellows. She pointed out many interesting places, and told him about the heroes who died in the war against Berserk. There was Queen Grace, the most beautiful and caring Mellow in the kingdom. She was eaten by a Snagon on the first day.

"I saw that happen in my vision, when I ate the yellow buds from the Tree of Past Times," Gregory explained. "That must have been a very sad day."

"Yes, it was," said Win, as she picked a purple flower and held it to his nose.

"What is this?" Gregory asked with a smile. The purple petals wrapped themselves gently around his nostrils. He could feel a pleasant sensation all over his body, but there was no fragrance from the flower.

"It is a Graote plant. We use them to make a soothing medicine."

Gregory felt good, but it had more to do with Win than the plant. She was very enchanting.

Win continued to explain the history of the Mellows. "Then there was Field Marshall Calm, who killed Wroth the brother of Berserk. Wroth was the mightiest warrior in their army, and his death sent King Berserk into a frenzy. He used all his effort to hunt him down, and when he caught Field Marshall Calm, he was skinned alive and fed to the Yarrags."

"Yarrags? What are they?" Gregory asked.

"They are smelly creatures with the body of a lion and the face of a hammer head shark. Berserk keeps them as his pets."

"I saw those in my vision too," said Gregory. "Thanks. I understand more about what I have seen now."

"Did you see General Humble in one of your visions?"

Gregory shrugged in response.

Win paused and beckoned him to sit down on a large coffee-coloured rock. "General Humble gave us the knowledge of how to kill a Bollof. Berserk's army use them to attack our lands. The General suffocated it by covering the hole in the Bolloff's back.

"Is it a big creature with the head of a dog and two horns?" Gregory asked.

"Yes, that's right," Win answered. "You have seen a lot."

Gregory sniffed the air. "What is that smell?" he asked.

"I was waiting for you to notice. We are at the Azucar Rocks. The rocks make the sweetest smell in the kingdom. I often come here to relax."

They sat talking a while longer.

"We better go back to the base now," said Win; and they made their way to meet with Placid.

Over in the land of the Feliroo, the Mellow ambassador and her guards had left Catabong Palace and were traveling back to the mountain city.

"Hold up. Wait for us," someone called out. It was Droll and Yord hopping towards them. Yord was still limping a little but had almost healed from his fall into the hole. The Mellow ambassador waited for them to catch up.

"Is there a problem Prince Droll?" she asked.

"We are coming with you to fight against Berserk," he replied.

"I tried to talk him out of it, but my brother is very stubborn," said Yord.

"What did your father say?" The ambassador asked. "We do not wish to offend the King."

"We did not ask for his permission." Droll answered, sounding annoyed. "You heard him; he is not interested in fighting, but we are."

"You are! I am only here to keep an eye on you so that you don't do anything stupid," said Yord.

The ambassador nodded her head in acknowledgement, and they continued their journey.

They travelled a few kilometres through herds of Akiti, talking about the weapons needed to bring Berserk's evil monarchy to an end. All the time they were being watched. Then the third who was on lookout saw a movement and raised her arm.

"Take cover!" she cried. But before they could run, they came under attack. The third was struck by an arrow and she fell to the floor. A rotating hammer flew into Yord's body, and his blood splattered onto Droll's arm.

In the blink of an eye, the two thirds holding the seat for the ambassador were also hit. The ambassador came crashing down to the earth and rolled in the dust.

Droll was devastated to see his brother lifeless on the floor, and charged towards the rocks to confront the attackers. Then he too was brought down. Blink-Speed had hit him with her hoof and now stood over him. "Someone help me tie them up," she said.

Porma slowly went over to where Yord's body lay and picked up his hammer. Luda apprehended the Mellow ambassador, and Yallon tied up Droll.

"What is their status?" Skrimp asked the Special Guard.

"They are all dead apart from these two," Blink-Speed replied.

"Bring the vermin." ordered Skrimp.

Porma picked up Droll and put him over his shoulder. Yallon picked up the ambassador and did the same. Then the Special Guard headed off back to Korfe Castle, leaving the others dead where they fell.

"We have done well. Our King will be pleased," said Skrimp. "Now we need to find the Fire Head."

Merew the torturer looked at Droll and the ambassador. "Leave the vermin to me. They will tell me where Fire Head is," she laughed bloodthirstily in excitement.

Elsewhere, King Berserk was walking his Yarrags through the castle garden. Manaso was ahead of him, holding his club. There were no flowers to be seen, only dried up bushes and weeds. The entire grounds were harsh and unforgiving. A reflection of King Berserk's reign and the darkness of his soul.

"My Lord," a voice called. King Berserk turned and saw one of his servants behind him. "Mediana is here, Your Majesty. Shall I send her out?"

"Tell her to wait. I will see her in the throne room."

"Yes, my Lord," said the servant as he hurried away to pass on the message.

King Berserk handed the lead to Manaso. The Yarrags were pulling and howling viciously. "Take them to their den," he said, and headed back to the inner castle.

Berserk approached the throne room where two guards stood protecting the entrance. "Send in the witch,' he told them.

They called Mediana, and her hologram appeared before the throne and bowed to the King.

"What news do you have for me, witch? I am running out of patience." He shuffled in his seat. "Where is the Fire Head and where is the Nactu?"

"The Fire Head is with the Feliroo, my Lord, and the Special Guard are on their way back here to make plans for war."

"The Feliroo! Griscat has betrayed me!" Berserk was livid. He called a guard, who came at once.

"Tell Manaso to gather the hunters. I am feeling hungry."

The guard nodded and left.

"What about the Nactu?" King Berserk asked Mediana.

"There is no sign of it, my Lord. I have visited the excavation site, and the whole area has been dug. They assured me that it is on the other side of the Tevro mountains on Feliroo land." Mediana explained.

"What are they waiting for? Tell them to go and dig there!"

"Yes, my Lord," said Mediana, and then her hologram vanished.

Once again, Berserk cleared the throne room of guards so that he could open the secret vault in the floor and take out the black box. He held it close to his chest and opened the lid.

There was a loud knock on the throne room door. "Your Majesty, I have brought you a gift," said Skrimp from behind the door.

"Wait" Berserk replied as he swiftly closed the box, set it back in the vault, and readjusted the throne. When he had finished, he told Skrimp to enter.

In walked Skrimp and the five remaining Special Guard. Over the shoulders of Porma and Yallon were the unconscious prince Droll and the Mellow ambassador.

"We were on our way back to the castle when we unexpectedly came across these two rats," Skrimp said with a scowl. She signalled to Porma and Yallon and they dumped their captives on the floor.

Berserk leapt up off the throne. "These treacherous fools dare to challenge me, King Berserk, the master of all. They are not worthy to kiss my feet." He looked at the two limp bodies on the floor. "For your treachery you will pay with your lives."

The King began to shake the band of torment, and the captives immediately woke up, screaming in pain.

"My Lord, they have information that we need," interrupted Skrimp.

The King lowered his hand. "Very well. Take them to the dungeons."

"Yes, my Lord," Skrimp replied. The Special Guard dragged Droll and the ambassador to the dungeons.

King Berserk went over to the statue of Queen Flora and placed his arms around its shoulders. "I am free from my promise to you, my love. Griscat has broken the treaty," he smiled, revealing his yellowed teeth.

Down in the dungeon, the Special Guard were with Droll and the Mellow ambassador in the pitch-black darkness of the torture chamber. Merew was eager to get started right away and took out her tools of punishment ready to extract information. She enjoyed inflicting suffering and was always brutal and cruel.

"Do not kill them until we have got what we want," ordered Skrimp. 'Start with the Feliroo vermin."

Porma flung Droll to the ground, then forcefully shackled his hands and feet to the wall. Droll struggled to break lose but it was pointless as the chains were too thick.

Skrimp commanded Yallon to force the Mellow ambassador to watch Droll's plight. She wanted to terrify her into revealing information about the Fire Head.

Merew the torturer began to laugh with glee as she went to work. Droll cried out in unbearable pain. The more he cried, the more she laughed.

"Where is the Fire Head?"

Droll did not answer, so she began to torture him again. Then Skrimp signalled for Merew to stop.

"That is enough for now."

Yallon dragged the ambassador to the wall next to Droll and chained her up.

Then Skrimp and the rest of the Special Guard went out of the room, leaving Droll moaning in the darkness of the chamber.

King Cordial lay sleeping a short distance away. Latip opened the door and entered. He was very distressed.

"Your Majesty," Latip whispered, "they have captured the ambassador and Prince Droll. Their fates are now sealed," he said sadly.

On hearing this, King Cordial looked up quickly and stared at Latip in disbelief. "What happened? Tell me what you know?"

"The Special Guard brought them in a short while ago and took them to the torture chamber.".

"We need to get them out before they are killed," said the King.

"How can we do that, Your Majesty? The castle is heavily fortified, and Berserk is even more paranoid than ever now that Fire Head has arrived."

"We must find a way, my friend," the King answered, deeply absorbed in his thoughts, trying to find a solution. "Have the fireworks been prepared for the magra service celebration next week Latip?"

"Yes, my King."

"Good, send a message to the mountain city and tell them we need a rescue party here immediately. Have them wait outside the city wall. Make sure the drawbridge is down when they arrive."

"Yes, my Lord," Latip said, and left the cell to have the message delivered.

Meanwhile, the news of the Mellow ambassador's capture had reached the mountain city, and the overriding feeling amongst the Mellows was dread.

The Mellow Council ordered an emergency meeting and asked for Gregory to be present. He promptly sat alongside Placid and listened keenly to the proceedings.

"We are here to discuss our strategy for dealing with the issue of the capture of the ambassador," said the chief elder. "What are your thoughts?"

There were many conflicting ideas from the executive. Some were pushing for an all-out attack; others suggested a more diplomatic approach.

Field Marshall Prudence would have none of it. "Are we forgetting who we are? Our King has ordered a rescue party to be sent, so that's what we should do. No more and no less. When the ambassador is safely within these walls we will decide how and when to attack," she said.

There was unanimous assent. The Mellow Council started to debate who should go as part of the rescue team.

Once again there were differing views. Some said it should be six rescuers, whilst others said it should be twelve. They eventually agreed that there should be twelve.

Field Marshall Prudence insisted that Gregory be part of the rescue team.

"We cannot send him. It is too early, said the chief elder.

"That's right. He may be injured or worse, killed," another chimed in.

"The prophecy says that he will lead us to victory, and that is our hope," said the Field Marshall.

There were still groans of discontent amongst the council.

"This is not an easy decision. Let us have a show of hands for all those who think that Gregory should go with the rescue party," said the chief elder. There were twelve hands raised.

"All those who think Gregory should stay raise your hands." Again, there were twelve hands raised.

"If I may," said Placid.

"Go ahead. Speak," said the leader.

"Why not let Gregory decide?" The Mellow Council looked around at one another, but everyone was silent.

"What do you think, Gregory. Are you ready?" The chief elder asked.

Gregory froze in fright for a moment, thinking of what could happen to him. Then he remembered Mezra's words.

"Yes, I am ready," he said nervously.

The chief elder closed the meeting and Gregory left with Placid to prepare for the rescue.

Meanwhile, over in the land of the Feliroo, King Griscat was dining with Queen Tabatha. "Do you know where Droll and Yord are?" The King asked as they were being served their meal. "I have not seen them all day."

Queen Tabatha sipped her beverage and broke some bread. "No," she said, and took a bite. The Queen loved her food, especially the Feliroo delicacy of Likoy, which was made from potato. "I have been asking for them myself. I do hope that they are not off getting into mischief. Droll is always looking for adventure and Yord follows behind him like an extra tail," she said.

The royal couple habitually listened to relaxing music when they dined. An instrumentalist stood nearby, playing a traditional Feliroo song on a finely crafted Rabilnot. The Rabilnot was an eight-stringed harp made from a local cactus plant, and produced notes that had soothing qualities. The musician wore a purple and gold sash with the royal crest.

As the King and Queen unwound, their dinner was interrupted by the sudden appearance of Themdar.

"Sorry for the intrusion," she said, and stood there with a downcast expression on her face. The music stopped abruptly. "What is it, Themdar?" The King asked.

Themdar began to open her mouth to speak, then closed it before any words came out. "Speak!" The King demanded, already knowing in his heart that something was seriously wrong.

"It is best that you come with me, Your Majesty," said Themdar.

The King rose from the table. "I will return shortly, my beloved," he said, kissing the Queen lovingly on her forehead. As Themdar and the King were leaving the dining room, the Queen suddenly stood up, "Have you seen my boys, Themdar?" she asked, with a feeling of dread.

On hearing her question, Themdar stopped in her tracks, but said nothing. "Answer me!" she shouted.

Themdar turned to the Queen with a painful look in her eyes and said slowly, "Queen Tabatha, I am sorry to have to inform you that Prince Yord is dead."

The Queen was panic-stricken at the devastating news and let out a heart wrenching scream. She was trembling with shock from head to toe. King Griscat rushed to comfort the Queen and caught her just as she was about to collapse. He held her arm as she sat back down on the chair.

The King continued to console her as she wept bitterly for prince Yord. "I am truly sorry, my King. I did not want to give you the news in front of the Queen," said Themdar.

"What happened?" the King asked roughly.

"It appears that both of the princes were with the Mellow ambassador heading for the mountain city. They were attacked by Berserk's Special Guard, Your Majesty. Prince Yord was murdered by Porma and his hammer. One of the Akiti farmers witnessed everything."

"What of Prince Droll?" the Queen asked through her tears. The King gently dried her weeping eyes with his handkerchief.

"Prince Droll was captured and taken to Berserk's palace, Your Majesty," Themdar informed them softly.

"Berserk will surely pay for this," King Griscat said, clutching the Queen's arm tightly. "Prepare the troops for war!"

"Yes, my Lord." Themdar rushed away to ready the Feliroo army.

THE RESCUE

Skrimp and the Special Guard were in the throne room with King Berserk. "My Lord, we will need to gather reinforcements to go to war with Griscat," she said.

"We are almost there, tiny one," Berserk said with a broad grin. "Find out all you can from the vermin in the dungeon and then dispose of them."

"Yes, my Lord," she beckoned the rest of the guards and started to head out.

BOOM. There was a massive explosion in the courtyard that shook the whole castle. The Special Guard were thrown to the floor by the force of the blast. King Berserk ducked for cover as series of small explosions started to set off in quick succession.

"Porma and Yallon, get the King to safety. The rest of you come with me," directed Skrimp.

Down below, Gregory, Placid and the rescue team were heading towards the torture chamber. There were flares and fireworks shooting off in all directions as they made their way swiftly through the courtyard, fending off several palace guards along the way. When they reached the door to the chamber, they smashed it down and went inside.

The ambassador and Droll made a pitiful sight chained up against the wall.

"Are you alright?" Captain Placid asked.

"I am fine," said the ambassador. "Prince Droll is badly injured."

Placid broke off the chains with her Nid. The ambassador and Droll were lifted and set on a seat between two thirds.

As the group were leaving, they came under attack from the Special Guard. Skrimp's arrow hit one of the thirds carrying the ambassador and she toppled over. Placid grabbed the seat and continued out of the courtyard.

Then she flung her Nid at Skrimp. It narrowly missed her but damaged a wall causing the debris to fly into her face.

Gregory took his opportunity and set the dial on his glasses to number five. *Whoosh!* He went to super speed and propelled himself at Skrimp. Blink-Speed saw what was happening and launched a counterattack at Gregory, intercepting him before he got to Skrimp. *CRASH!* There was an almighty collision as Gregory and Blink-Speed bounced off each other in opposite directions.

The fireworks were still exploding around them in the palace. Placid called out to Gregory and he shot off in her direction. He caught up with her in seconds, and they carried on at speed with Droll and the ambassador. Gregory suddenly felt a pain at the side off his head. He tried to carry on running, but blacked out and fell on the floor. Placid loaded him onto the seat and carried them all to the haven of the mountain city.

Back at the castle infirmary, Skrimp was in bed. She had been blinded in one eye by the debris.

"Where are they?" she asked angrily.

"They got away," said Blink-Speed.

"Where is King Berserk?"

"He is safe."

"How did the vermin get in?"

"The Fire Head was with them," Blink-Speed said nervously.

"I shot him. Did you find his body?" Skrimp asked expectantly.

"No, we found nothing."

Skrimp got up. "We must search the perimeters," commanded Skrimp. They both left the infirmary.

In the throne room, King Berserk was with Luda, Yallon, Merew and Porma. "How did they escape?" he shouted. "We must crush them once and for all!"

A guard entered the room. "Your Majesty, Mediana is here."

"Send her in," said the King.

Mediana's hologram appeared. "We have found it, my Lord. We have the Nactu."

"Bring it to me at once," he said ecstatically.

"It is on the way, Your Majesty."

"Good work, witch," he said rubbing his hands together.

At that moment, Skrimp and Blink-Speed also entered the throne room.

"You are wounded, tiny one," said the King as he saw the patch on Skrimp's eye.

"I am fine, my Lord."

"We must prepare for war. The time is at hand to destroy these vermin for good," said Berserk, hungry for blood.

"What about the reinforcements?" Skrimp asked.

"We will soon have all the reinforcements we need."

Berserk began to laugh.

Down in the dungeons, Latip was with King Cordial. The sounds of the commotion still clearly audible in the outer courtyard. "We did it, Your Majesty. We managed to free the ambassador and Prince Droll," he said excitedly.

"That is excellent Latip."

"There's a bit of bad news," Latip continued with a worried expression on his face. "Fire Head may have been hit."

"Let me know as soon as you know more,' said King Cordial.

"Yes, my Lord,"

Latip turned and left the dungeon.

Over at Catabong Palace, King Griscat and the Feliroo nation performed the burial service of Prince Yord. It was their custom that the body should be buried within twenty-four hours unless the cause of death was unknown. The funeral was a magnificent event, with all the pomp and pageantry befitting a member of the royal household.

The entire Feliroo nation were present: royals; dignitaries; peasants; and farmers. It was a time of great sadness throughout the kingdom, as they lined the streets to pay their respect.

As soon as the ceremony finished, King Griscat took his place at the head of the army. They gathered at the statue of the Iron Fork. This was the place where many famous Feliroo battles were won. They left from the statue and began a slow march towards the Kingdom of Rage.

Meanwhile, Gregory woke in the rest zone in the mountain city. "Ouch!" He cried out as he felt the side of his face. There was a bandage covering it.

At that point, Win entered the rest zone. "Calm down Gregory. You are going to be just fine. You were hit during the rescue, but it is only a graze."

"What about the ambassador and Droll?" Gregory asked.

"They are here, safe and well. You should be proud," said Win.

Gregory had a strange feeling something was not right. He felt his head again. He was not wearing his glasses. A feeling of dread overwhelmed him. "Where are my glasses?" he asked, anxiously scanning the room but not seeing them anywhere.

"I don't know. Maybe they took them off to dress your wound."

"I need them," Gregory said in a panic, feeling the bed around him with both of his hands. *They were not there!*

"Okay, relax, I will look in your backpack." Win picked it up from the end of the bed and searched through it.

"Are they there?" Gregory asked restlessly.

"No, they are not. I will call Captain Placid." Win put her hand on his shoulder reassuringly. He lay back down on the pillow, and she left the rest zone. After a short while Win returned with the captain.

"What is the problem, Fire Head?"

"Where are my glasses?" he tried to sit up, but a sharp pain shot down the side of his cheek.

"Your glasses came off as we left Korfe Castle."

Gregory's heart sank, "I must find them. How long have I been here in the city?"

"About four hours. Why?"

"How long did it take us to get back here from the castle?" he asked.

"Around two hours. What is this all about?" Placid looked at him strangely.

"If I don't find the glasses in the next six hours, it is all over."

"What do you mean?"

"Before I came on this task, Mezra told me that I should never remove the glasses for more than twelve hours."

"What will happen if you do?" asked Placid.

"The pledge will be broken, and the power of the magic glasses lost forever," he said.

"When you collapsed outside of the palace you were not wearing them. I think that an arrow may have hit the side of the glasses. They could have fallen anywhere." Placid said.

Gregory slumped on the bed, deep in thought.

"We shall do our best to find them, but we must be realistic. Berserk may have them already, Fire Head." said the captain.

Back at Korfe Castle, Blink-Speed, Merew, Luda, Porma and Yallon were looking for Gregory outside the walls. They scoured the entire area but could not find any sign of him. Luda called Blink-Speed, "I have found these strange tracks here," she pointed to the dusty ground where there were small marks that led to a bush. "Shall I follow them?"

"We don't have time for this," said Blink-Speed. "We have wasted enough time already. Let's get back to the King."

When they reached the throne room they waited until called inside. King Berserk was sitting on the throne, with Skrimp and Manaso standing by his side. "We scoured the perimeters as you asked, but there was no sign of Fire Head," said Blink-Speed.

"Don't worry, we will have our day with him and the rest of the scum," promised Skrimp.

The throne room went quiet as Ret walked in. In his hand was something wrapped up in a scarlet cloth. He bowed his head and approached the throne. King Berserk's eyes opened wide as he took the cloth from Ret's hand. He carefully opened the material, and there was the Wand of Nactu! It was making a strange sound and the occupants of the room were mesmerised.

"We are ready now," King Berserk said.

Back at the mountain city things were getting desperate for Gregory. It had been eleven hours since he lost the magic glasses, and no one could find them. Captain Placid had gone to retrace their path but found nothing. Latip had looked around the castle grounds, courtyard, and the inner wall, but could not locate them either.

The atmosphere was dreary as hope drained away from the Mellows. Gregory tried to remain up-beat and spoke to Win, giving her some of the things in his backpack. She was very intrigued by the gifts, but concern was clearly written on her face.

Gregory took his harmonica and began to play a sad song. There were several Mellows in his rest zone, including Captain

Placid. Nobody spoke a word; and when he had finished playing, he said his goodbyes.

According to his calculations, he had about ten minutes before he would disappear back to his mum's house, and the magic glasses would be lost forever.

"What's going on here? Did somebody die?" A small voice asked.

"Now is not the time, Wedger," said Gregory.

"What's the matter, Fire Head. Ain't you pleased to see me?" Gregory looked down at Wedger and his heart leapt in his chest. He was dragging the magic glasses behind him. "What the heck, Wedger. You have saved the day." Everyone began to cheer and there were smiles all round.

Placid picked up the glasses, made a few adjustments, and put them on Gregory's face. The Mellows were hugging and patting each other on the back.

"What about me?" Wedger said.

Gregory placed him on his shoulder.

"How did you find them?"

"I was in your backpack on the rescue mission just in case you needed some help. When you got shot by the arrow, I saw the glasses slip off your face. So, I jumped down and got them."

"You mean, you dragged them all the way from the palace to here, Wedger?"

"That's right, big fella. I know how ugly you are without them."

They both began to laugh.

"Seriously Wedger, you are a hero," said Gregory.

"That's the least I could do. You saved my life. I nearly got caught by the Special Guard," said Wedger. "I had to hide behind a bush. Their tracker picked up my trail, but for some reason they never followed it. I was only a few feet away from them, but they turned back. It was close."

'You are very courageous, Wedger,' said Gregory, relieved to be able to remain in the book realm.

"We have no time to lose, we need to attack Berserk. Our sources at Korfe Castle tell us that he has the Wand of Nactu in his possession. It is only a matter of time before he uses it," interrupted Captain Placid.

"What is the Wand of Nactu?" Gregory enquired.

"It is an ancient weapon used to raise the dead. Berserk will head an unstoppable evil army if we do not act soon."

A breathless guard entered the rest zone.

"Captain Placid I have news. King Griscat and the Feliroo army have been seen marching towards Korfe Castle."

"Send a messenger to intercept them and tell King Griscat that Prince Droll is safe with us in the mountain city," said Placid. The guard immediately turned and left.

Back at the dungeon in Korfe Castle, Latip sat with King Cordial. The door burst open and Skrimp entered with Blink-Speed and Porma. "Seize him!" Skrimp barked. Porma grabbed Latip and put him over his shoulder.

"What is the meaning of this?" King Cordial protested.

"We know he is your spy Cordial. He is going to pay the price."

They carried Latip out of the cell and took him to the torture chamber. Merew was waiting there ready for action. Once again, she had her tools laid out on the table. They strapped Latip to the wall and began to ask him questions. He refused to answer them, so Merew went to work on him, and his screams could be heard ringing through the outer corridor. They did not last long before the place went eerily quiet.

Skrimp and Blink-Speed come out of the chamber. "Merew is too eager," said Skrimp, as they headed for the throne room. When they reached there King Berserk was in a heated debate with Mediana's hologram.

"We need to raise them now!" he cried, pushing over a marble stand that hit the ground with a 'Crash' as it cracked the floor tile.

"My Lord, Latip is dead," said Skrimp.

'What! I told you to make him suffer."

"He was weak, my Lord. He could not take the pressure," lied Skrimp.

"So be it," said the King "I have more important things at hand."

'What shall we do with the body, my Lord?"

"We will make an example of this snake. Take him to the courtyard and tell Manaso to let the Yarrags eat." Berserk ordered.

"Yes, my Lord," said Skrimp leaving with Blink-Speed.

Berserk and Mediana continued their conversation. "Now we are preparing, my Lord. All will soon be ready. The 'raising of the dead ceremony' needs to take place at the Tevro burial ground. We cannot do it at the castle."

The King revealed his displeasure with an angry grunt.

"Then Tevro it is. Leave me, witch."

With that the hologram faded. Berserk reclined on the throne. As he was gathering his sinister thoughts, a guard knocked on the throne room door.

"Enter!"

The guard rushed in and bowed before the King.

"Your Majesty, King Griscat and his army have been seen at the edge of the kingdom."

"What!" Berserk cried. "Call the Special Guard. We go to Tevro!"

"Yes, my Lord."

The guard scurried out.

In the mountain city, the Mellows were preparing for war. Gregory spoke with Captain Placid. "Why did we not save King Cordial when we were at the Palace?"

"Berserk performed witchcraft. He took King Cordial's heart from his body and hid it somewhere. If the King leaves the courts of the palace without his heart he will surely die," said Placid.

"You mean he has literally taken his heart? We need to get it back," said a shocked Gregory.

One of the Mellow Patrol entered with a sad look on her face. "Latip is dead," she said. Placid stood silent for a few seconds. "What happened?"

"He was arrested for spying, and the Special Guard tortured him to death."

Placid bowed her head. "He was a real soldier for the kingdom. How is King Cordial?"

"The King is well," said the third.

"Good," said Captain Placid with a relieved expression on her face.

Meanwhile, outside the mountain city, the Feliroo army were camped in the valley. King Griscat had received news that prince Droll was with the people of Mellow and had travelled to meet him. Themdar and a small company of guards were led inside the mountain city. They were taken directly to the main hall where the twenty-four elders of the Mellow Council were waiting.

All the Mellows stood and bowed when King Griscat entered.

"Welcome, Your Majesty," said the chief elder.

"Where is my son?" The King asked with urgency in his voice. "I want to see him."

"Of course, Your Majesty," said the elder, "Placid, escort the King to Prince Droll."

Placid and Gregory led King Griscat and Themdar to the rest zone where prince Droll was recovering.

The prince was awake when they entered.

"Father!" he cried out with his arms open wide. The King instantly responded by running to his son and they hugged each other tightly.

"Yord is dead. We were attacked," Droll said still traumatised.

"I know, my son," said the King as Droll wept onto his shoulder. "Your brother's death will be avenged."

"It was my fault. I should have stayed in Geba," said Droll through his tears.

"No, my son, it is not your fault. There is only one person to blame for this and he will pay for his wickedness." King Griscat said softly.

THE SIDES

King Berserk stood at a podium in Tevro at the Gantmas burial site, surrounded by thousands of troops and the remaining Special Guard. His slaves were also among them, dressed in their grey tunics. The King carried the powerful Wand of Nactu. He wore a smug look on his face.

"Today is the day we rid ourselves of these vermin!" he shouted to his followers, who cheered with enthusiasm waving their shields in the air.

"Too long we have let them freely roam the land. Now is the time to exterminate them!"

The baying crowd roared even louder.

"Where is the witch?" he asked, looking around at those closest to him. Mediana stepped forward, holding an ancient parchment in her hands. "Here I am my Lord."

"Good, let us begin,"

Berserk raised his arms whilst the crowd frantically cheered. He waited a while and then lowered them, and the cheering stopped abruptly. There was complete silence as Mediana held up the parchment and began to read.

"Oh, soldiers of the grave, I call you. Rise and stand before your King. Wake up from your deathly slumber and heed his commands. He is the one who holds the Nactu and directs its power. It is time to arise!"

Mediana then began to speak in an unknown language.

Berserk raised the Nactu into the air. The ground started to tremor like a small earthquake. At the sound of rocks crashing together beneath the earth, the masses cried out in fear.

"Silence!" Berserk yelled.

All those who cried out ceased to open their mouths. Then the earth began to spit out the evil army of the dead. They rose like worms from the ground, their grotesque half-rotten bodies holding the weapons of war that they fell with. The soldiers carried the marks and scars they had sustained during their lifetimes.

They all rose erect and ready for battle. In no time at all there were thousands of risen dead soldiers standing to attention all around the burial site. King Berserk laughed, and his army started to cheer again.

Skrimp turned to the King. "With this army you will be invincible. Who can stand against you?"

Berserk nodded his big head and continued to laugh.

"No one can," he boasted. "Kill the Slaves," he ordered.

Some of his soldiers ran and set upon them. "*Gak*" was the sound made by the slaves whilst being choked to death. The others cried out in pain as they were sliced and bludgeoned until they were lifeless. Ret had a look of disbelief on his face as he was impaled on a soldier's spear. The killing did not stop until all the slaves who worked at the burial ground were dead.

"Your Majesty, we may have had need of them," Mediana said.

"They are of no use to me now that we have the Nactu," said Berserk.

"Yes, my Lord," she replied.

In the Kingdom of Rage mercy did not exist. Only violence and cruelty were permitted by order of the King.

King Berserk was ready to step up the level of treachery to feed his insatiable appetite for power. All those around him knew that no one was safe from his paranoia and selfish ambition.

"The times has come to go and destroy the Feliroo," he said; and with that the army of Rage, consisting of the living and the dead, headed off to the land of Geba to seize Catabong Palace.

In the meantime, back in the mountain city, the Mellow Council sat with King Griscat. Placid and Gregory were also with them. "I wish to thank you for rescuing my son. I am forever in your debt," said Griscat'.

"You are welcome, Your Majesty," said the chief elder. "Now we need to turn our attention to Berserk."

"Agreed, let us attack the castle from all sides so none can escape," said the King. As he was speaking a third came in and whispered in the chief elder's ear. She rose from her seat with a shocked look on her face and turned to speak to King Griscat.

"Your Majesty, we need to move now. Berserk and his soldiers are on the other side of the Tevro in the Gantmas burial grounds."

Everyone looked at each other in stunned horror.

"He has managed to raise an army of the dead," the chief elder continued.

"We need to secure the mountain city," said one of the elders.

"That won't be necessary. They are not marching in this direction but are heading the opposite way," said the chief elder

"They are going to attack our land," said King Griscat. "We must leave at once and head them off."

Everyone hurriedly departed from the hall at his order.

"Why are Berserk's army not coming here? They are so close?" Gregory asked.

"They will leave us until last. Berserk knows we will not attack him while he has King Cordial's heart. We need to do something fast," said Placid.

"What do you mean?" Gregory asked.

"Before he had the army of the dead, he was not as strong and needed to keep King Cordial as a bargaining tool. Now there is no reason to keep him alive."

"Then we must get the King and his heart back at once," said Gregory.

"How are we going to do that?" Placid asked.

"I have an idea," Gregory said.

They both continued talking as they left the hall. After their conversation, Captain Placid gathered the Mellow infantry and joined King Griscat's soldiers. Gregory and six of the Mellow Patrol headed for Korfe Castle to free King Cordial and retrieve his heart.

King Griscat, Placid and their two armies set off to pursue and destroy Berserk's soldiers before they reached the Feliroo capital. They moved swiftly across the land with a fierce determination, knowing that this was going to be an apocalyptic battle that would change history forever.

Meanwhile, Gregory and the Mellow Patrol were racing en route to Korfe Castle. He had butterflies in his stomach as they got close to its outer walls.

"Get down, I hear a noise," said one of the thirds.

They all ducked and hid behind some bushes.

When Gregory peeped around the leaves, he saw that King Berserk and a battalion of his regular soldiers were outside the castle, waiting for the drawbridge to come down. With them were Blink-Speed, Yallon and Merew from the Special Guard.

"Stay here and watch for my signal," said Gregory.

The Mellow Patrol nodded in response. Then he clicked the switch on his glasses to become invisible and ran to catch up to the battalion before they entered the castle gates. The drawbridge lowered, and the huge gates opened. Gregory walked through with the marching soldiers, making his way to the front, to be within ear shot of Berserk and the Special Guard.

"Bring the King of the vermin to me," said Berserk.

"Yes, my Lord," said Blink-Speed before leaving with Yallon and Merew to go to the dungeons.

Berserk commanded the battalion to stop and wait in the castle courtyard. Then he continued to the throne room escorted by two of the palace guards.

Invisible, Gregory walked quietly behind them. When they reached the throne room doors, Berserk ordered the guards to stay outside, and he entered in alone.

Gregory took his chance and turned the dial on his glasses to super speed. He whizzed into the throne room just before the doors closed. They were alone and he stood perfectly still against a wall, waiting to see what Berserk would do. He watched as Berserk went over to the statue of Queen Flora and kissed it on the lips. Then, laughing maniacally, he walked swiftly to the throne and dragged it from the tiles to retrieve the black box.

"Today you will feel my power, vermin. You will taste pain like never before."

He continued to laugh as he opened the lid of the box, revealing a large jar containing a beating heart.

Gregory was shocked and stepped back in amazement. '*SNAP*'. He looked down. He had trodden on a small twig.

"Who is here?" Berserk asked. "I heard you. Come out, wherever you are," he demanded angrily.

Gregory was glued to the spot in fear. His heart was beating nervously as he tried to figure out what to do.

Then Berserk came towards him still holding the jar in his hand.

"I can hear you. Show yourself!" he screamed, foaming at the mouth. Berserk raised his arm, ready to inflict the band of torment.

Gregory ran and snatched the jar from his hand.

"Guards!" shouted Berserk, and they immediately came running in. Gregory zoomed past them through the door and headed for the dungeon. He was almost there when he saw Blink-Speed, Merew the torturer, and Yallon in the courtyard coming towards him with King Cordial. The King was in handcuffs, and they were dragging him along.

In a split-second, Gregory whacked Blink-Speed, causing her to fall backward and hit her head. She was knocked out cold and lay on the floor.

Merew stood there in shock. Yallon looked at the unconscious Blink-Speed and started hitting the air with his sword.

"Show yourself coward. I will chop you to pieces," Yallon said angrily.

He was too big for Gregory to knock over with speed, so he turned the dial on his glasses to number eleven and started to grow.

In no time at all he became a giant. Gregory bent down, grabbed Yallon, and threw him at Merew. She was crushed against the wall with Yallon on top of her.

Then Gregory picked up King Cordial with his right hand and put him in his pocket. He ran through the battalion of soldiers, who were still standing in the courtyard, and knocked them over like skittles with his giant feet.

Berserk stormed onto his balcony in a fit of rage.

"Stop him," he cried out to the soldiers.

The battalion were in a state of confusion, seeing nothing around them but fallen comrades. They did not know who to fight.

Gregory climbed over the palace wall with ease and headed towards the bushes where the thirds were hiding. He put King Cordial down carefully.

"Here is the King's heart," he said, handing it to one of the thirds. "Now get his Majesty back to the mountain city as fast as possible. I will buy you some time."

The thirds headed for the security of the mountain fortress with King Cordial. Gregory ran over to Korfe Castle just in time as the soldiers were opening the gate. He lifted the drawbridge and put his huge back against it to keep it from opening. On the other side, the soldiers were trapped inside trying to push the drawbridge down, but it would not budge.

"What is going on?" Berserk roared. "Open it. Push it down, you fools," he cried. But they could not.

Then Yallon got up off the floor and looked at Merew the torturer. She was dead, his heavy frame had crushed her to death against the wall when Gregory threw him. Now there were only four Special Guard left.

Yallon cried out in anger and made his way to the front of the battalion and began to push the drawbridge.

"Help them," Berserk screamed. And more soldiers joined them in the effort.

Gregory struggled to keep the castle drawbridge closed. His arms were stretched out to their limit and his hands were gripping tightly onto the slippery stone walls.

"The drawbridge is moving," cried Yallon, as it opened slightly.

"Push harder," shouted Berserk, who was still on the balcony.

"I am pushing as hard as I can," said Yallon through gritted teeth.

Gregory was determined to give the thirds as much time as possible to get away from the castle. He dug his feet into the moat and with a mighty effort slammed the drawbridge back shut. This caused Yallon, and the soldiers to fall backwards.

Berserk called Manaso to him. "Take the Yarrags through the hidden passage and let them loose on the intruder."

Manaso nodded and left.

"Push it open," Berserk yelled to the others.

Yallon and the soldiers began to push once again.

Apart from King Berserk, Manoso was the only one who could handle the Yarrags without being eaten. They had gobbled up many guards who were foolish enough to get too close to them.

Manaso went to where they were confined in the bowels of the palace and opened the door. They roared and growled, roaming around the large, circular den. The vicious creatures were attached to the wall by two long, strong, and extremely thick chains.

He unhooked them from the wall and wrapped the chains around his arms to shorten their leash. The Yarrags were snapping and growling, but reluctantly followed him through the dark labyrinth of tunnels below the castle to a hidden door.

Manaso pushed it and they went through. The door opened onto the side of the castle walls behind some bushes, next to the moat. There was a little boat hidden there. Manaso boarded it with the Yarrags and set out to cross the water. The vessel nearly sank with all their weight, and they just about made it across.

Meanwhile, Gregory was still holding off the efforts of Yallon and the soldiers. Manaso led the Yarrags to the front of the palace and they began to go wild as they picked up Gregory's scent. The savage creatures were released, and they attacked Gregory ferociously biting at his enormous ankle. The pain was too much for him, so he shook them off and sent them flying.

He began to run, taking massive strides away from the castle. Yallon and the soldiers poured across the drawbridge, throwing spears, and firing sling shots; but Gregory was out of range. He turned around mid-flight and saw that the Yarrags were up and charging after him. Then he watched on as they were accidently killed by a huge boulder fired from a castle catapult.

"'No! They are not the target!" Yallon screamed.

Gregory kept running. Then, when he was a long distance away, he made himself normal size, then stopped to treat his wounds. The bites were quite small but very deep. He took some sterile wipes from his backpack to clean them and then bandaged his ankle.

"That was exciting," said Wedger, as he popped his head out of the backpack. "We showed them who's boss," he chuckled.

"What the heck, Wedger. You startled me." Gregory clutched his chest.

"Are you okay, big fella?" Wedger asked.

"My heart is still beating so fast. I just need a rest," said Gregory as he sat down and leaned back against a rock. After a short while, he put Wedger
in the backpack and continued to the safety of the mountain city.

Over by the Spongey Lake, close to the land of the Feliroo, Mediana, Skrimp, Luda and Porma were leading the army to destroy Catabong Palace.
The army consisted of cavalry, foot soldiers and many supply wagons. As they got closer to the Feliroo border they could see vast flocks of Akiti grazing in the valley.
"Remember, we do not stop for Akiti now. They are to be collected and put into the wagons on the way back." Mediana said as she noticed Skrimp watching them.
"I know that witch," Skrimp retorted with a glare. She had little time for Mediana and resented the fact that Berserk had given her command of the dead warriors. Skrimp was to oversee the regular Rage army. As they rode towards the land of Geba, Skrimp and Mediana travelled in an uncomfortable silence.
Gregory had reached the mountain city by this time and was speaking with some of the elders. "How is King Cordial?" he asked.
"His Majesty is well. You have done a great service for our people today." the elder responded.
"Thank you! Now I need to help to catch up with King Griscat and the others," Gregory said humbly.

"You are injured. Rest a while before you go," said another elder.

"I must join the battle now. I came here to ask for some Mellows to show me the way to Catabong Palace."

"So be it."

The elder called for two thirds to escort him. "Paz and Dashom take Gregory to King Griscat," he said.

"Yes, elder," they said in unison.

"Thank you," said Gregory.

The small party left the elders. On their way out Win came to meet them looking excited.

"Are you leaving now?" she asked.

"Yes, there is no time to lose," said Gregory.

"Let me come with you," asked Win.

"The battlefield is no place for you Win," said Gregory.

"I can fight," she explained.

"No, please stay here. We will speak when I return."

Win did not reply but had a disappointed look on her face.

"Please understand Win," said Gregory.

"Fight well," she said; then walked away.

Gregory and the two thirds left the mountain city and began their journey.

After a few minutes one of the thirds stopped.

"What's the matter?" Gregory asked.

"We are being followed," said the third, looking over at some boulders. "Over there in the rocks."

"Come out and show yourself, and we will spare your life," Gregory shouted.

"It is me," a familiar voice cried back. Win came out from her hiding place.

"What are you doing Win?" Gregory said in an annoyed tone. "It is not safe for you out here."

"I will be okay. I can take care of myself." she said confidently. Gregory was just about to respond when one of the thirds cried out.

"Snagon overhead!"

The beast swooped down and grabbed Win with its talons and began to take off with her. Gregory turned his glasses to super speed and shot over to the Snagon. He managed to grab hold of her legs and desperately tried to pull Win from the Snagon's clutches, but it was no use. As he struggled to set her free, he lost his grip and plummeted back down to the ground. Win screamed as the Snagon carried her away into the distance.

Gregory sat speechless on the ground. Tears began to trickle down his cheeks and anger overtook him.

"Are you okay, Fire Head?" one of the thirds approached Gregory.

"No, I am not," he snapped, as he wiped the tears from his face. "We need to join King Griscat as quickly as possible."

"There is a shortcut to the land of the Feliroo," said the third.

"No, that is not possible, Paz. It would be suicide to go through the Trubabox," said the other third.

"That is the only way to save time, Dashom," Paz replied.

"You are right, but we may not come out alive," said Dashom.

"We need to do it. We have no time to waste," said Gregory. He and Paz started to leave but Dashom hesitated.

"Come on, Dashom," Paz said.

Dashom reluctantly set off with them.

Meanwhile, over on the outskirts of Tevro, King Griscat led the coalition army. Alongside him were Themdar and Placid, travelling at a steady pace towards Catabong Palace. As they reached Feliroo land the group were approached by an Akiti farmer who was clearly in distress.

"Stop where you are and state your business farmer," Themdar cried out.

The farmer fell to his knees.

"Your Majesty, there is a terrible army of the dead ahead of you. They are just beyond those hills," he said urgently.

King Griscat looked at Captain Placid "Take some of the thirds and hold them up until we reach you. They must not be allowed to reach Catabong Palace," he ordered.

The thirds could move twice as fast as the Feliroo. There was no time to lose as Griscat did not want Berserk's army to breach the palace defences.

"Yes, Your Majesty," said Placid.

"You are a noble one, Captain, for you may not make it out alive," said Griscat.

"Then we will die well," said Captain Placid with a faint smile. She gathered her troops and then set off with a battalion of a thousand thirds to intercept the army of the risen dead. They were travelling fast through the lush land of the Feliroo.

Gregory, Dashom and Paz had reached the Trubabox. They stood on a hill overlooking the crazy river Riomos. It was two rivers rolled into one. The water flowed in opposite directions, like a road with two lanes of traffic. One half had very fast-flowing, yellow water: the other had high red waves that travelled much slower. Gregory was staring at the water with a look of consternation.

"You cannot swim across. It will snap you in half before you get to the middle," said Dashom.

"That is not a problem for Gregory," Paz boasted.

"It may not be a problem for him, but what about us?" Dashom said.

Gregory smiled. "It will not be a problem for any of us." He turned the dial on his glasses to number eleven and began to grow. When he was gigantic, Gregory picked up Paz and Dashom and began to run towards the river. After a few steps he was at the water's edge. He took an enormous leap across to the other side.

The ground shook as his hefty frame landed on the riverbank. Gregory turned his attention to the land ahead of him which was made up of thousands of square blue boxes.

"You need to shrink," Paz shouted up at him.

"Why?" Gregory asked. "It is easier if I carry you both; we will get there quicker."

"No, you cannot cross the Trubabox that size. We will all surely die," said a worried Dashom.

"He is right," said Paz.

Gregory put them both safely on the ground. He then turned the dial and shrank back down to normal.

"Now what do we do?" he asked.

"We must find our path across the Trubabox without stepping on the wrong boxes," said Dashom.

They cautiously made their way over to the sea of boxes and stood at the edge.

"I will lead. Gregory should be at the back," said Paz.

"Okay," Dashom conceded.

"Do exactly what I do and follow my path," said Paz and they started to cross. He put his foot on a box and tested it with his toe. The box turned green, so he stood on it and tested another box before standing on it. Dashom and Gregory followed carefully behind him.

He continued to do this, leaving a trail of green boxes until suddenly, a box he stood on erupted. Red lava shot Paz high up in the air. He was screaming in agony as he disintegrated into liquid.

Gregory and Dashom ran back along the trail of green boxes as fast as they could go until they were safely back on the bank. They both fell onto the ground in shock.

"What will we do now?" Gregory asked.

"We must continue," said Dashom.

They got up and walked around the edge of the sea of boxes. When they were some distance away from the lava geyser Dashom stopped.

"Let's try here," he said, tentatively touching a nearby box with his foot.

"No, wait!" said Gregory.

"What's the problem?' Dashom asked.

"There must be another way. Let me think."

Gregory sat on the ground and Dashom joined him.

"We are wasting time by sitting here," said Dashom. Gregory didn't answer as he was deep in thought.

After a few seconds he stood up and looked at the sea of boxes. He turned the magic glasses setting to four, but nothing happened. Number five was super-speed, so he skipped that and went to setting six and looked out over the boxes.

Suddenly, he observed a pattern through the boxes. "I can see a way through!" Gregory said excitedly, but Dashom did not understand him. He turned the dial back to three.

"What's going on? Are you okay?" Dashom asked.

"I have found a way through. Follow me." Gregory recognised all the boxes that were safe to stand on. The glasses had given him the power to work out puzzles. Gregory led Dashom confidently through the ocean of boxes.

THE BATTLE

Queen Tabatha was in her chamber deep within Catabong Palace. There was a knock at the door.

"Your Majesty, we must leave quickly. Berserk's army are at the Iron Fork," said one of her guards.

"You know what you must do," she replied, as her handmaids hastily prepared the Queen's possessions before they travelled to the back of the palace to escape.

The guard rushed the opposite way to the courtyard at the front, and called to a soldier who was at the top of the watch tower. "Attack!"

The watchman pulled out a signal mirror and shone it at the hills a short distance away.

Five battalions of eliteT Feliroo guards began to stream out of the hills with a fierce war cry. They met Berserk's army of the risen dead head on.

The battle was fierce; javelins, swords, hatchets, and axes were wielded without mercy. Both sides inflicting death and injury on each other with equal vigour. Then a darkness covered the Feliroo sky as a group of fifty Snagons flew over Catabong Palace dropping huge boulders.

The walls and towers began to crumble during the onslaught as Queen Tabatha and her entourage fled. She was almost hit by an enormous rock that landed inches away from her. They all fell to the ground at the force of the impact.

Queen Tabatha stood up and her handmaids dusted her down. As they did so, she blew into an amulet whistle around her neck. After a short while thousands of tiny Keren birds took to the sky from every direction.

As they flew higher, the sky became pitch black. There were so many Kerens, they blocked the daylight. The birds began to fly into the mouths of the Snagons and down their throats, causing them to drop from the sky.

Then Queen Tabatha and her consort speedily continued their journey away from Catabong Palace as the battle raged on. The Snagons kept falling.

Mediana, Skrimp, Luda and Porma were on the outside of the battle, heading for the palace.

A short way behind them, Placid and her battalion had reached the heart of the Iron Fork. They launched themselves at the army of the dead. Captain Placid fought ferociously whilst scanning for Berserk or any of his Special Guard.

Over in the distance, she noticed a small band of people heading towards the palace. It was Mediana, Skrimp, Luda and Porma. Captain Placid called several of her soldiers and headed off after them.

"We need to kill Griscat," said Mediana to Skrimp as they entered through the palace gates.

"Agreed, let us split up. We will find him more easily," Skrimp said. They both parted ways. Mediana took Luda, and Skrimp left with Porma searching separate sections of the palace.

Simultaneously, Gregory and Dashom were trudging their way across the Trubabox. The sea of boxes finally ended, and they headed towards the sand dunes.

"We are almost there. Catabong Palace is just over that hill," said Dashom.

"That's great, I hope that we are not too late," said Gregory.

As he spoke, a giant Sand Serpent rose out of the ground poised to attack them. They were both terrified and tumbled down the dunes. The creature lunged at Gregory, but he had already turned his dial to super speed and began to run, leaving the creature far behind him.

Dashom was also moving fast to get away from the serpent.

On the other side of the dunes, Queen Tabatha and her convoy were heading towards Gregory. She was making her way to the Trubabox and aimed to escape to the mountain city.

Gregory ran over the dunes and came face to face with the convoy.

Queen Tabatha's guard began to throw javelins and axes at Gregory, who ran in a zig zag to avoid being hit.

"Stop!" Dashom shouted from the top of a dune.

The Feliroo guards stopped firing as soon as they saw that Dashom was a Mellow. Gregory also stopped running and the Feliroo stared at him open mouthed.

"It is Fire Head. The legend is true," said one of the guards.

Dashom caught up with Gregory and they stood together a few metres away from the Queen and her consort.

"That is Queen Tabatha," Dashom informed Gregory.

They walked over to the Queen and bowed.

"I am Gregory Your Majesty, and this is Dashom. We are at your service."

Before the Queen could answer, they came under attack. One of the Feliroo guards was hit by a hammer. It was the Itey of Porma smashing into him. The force sent him crashing to the ground. Then a second guard was felled by Skrimp's arrow.

Gregory twisted his dial and began to grow while Dashom threw her Nid at Porma. It hit him hard and was embedded in his shoulder. Porma fell to the ground, and Dashom ran over to where he lay and finished him off. Now there were only three of the Special Guard left.

Skrimp set her aim at Dashom and unleashed another arrow. Dashom was hit in the chest and fell to the ground lifeless. Skrimp turned her attention to Gregory, who was now a giant, and lined up the cross hairs of her Drad with Gregory's eye.

Just as she was about to fire, she was hit by a Nid which completely severed her arm from her body. As it dropped down at her feet, still holding the Drad, she cried out in pain and looked around to see who had attacked her. Placid stood in the distance.

Gregory hurried over to help Dashom but she was dead. He turned his attention to Skrimp who was trying to run away. Gregory took a few whopping strides and scooped up Skrimp in his hand.

"Wait here!" he called out to Placid.

Gregory made himself invisible and ran towards the Trubabox. Once he was beyond the dunes he began to shout.

"What are you doing?" Skrimp asked.

Then she saw a giant Sand Serpent heading towards them. Gregory dropped Skrimp on the sand and headed off speedily back to Queen Tabatha. He could hear Skrimp's distant scream as he crossed the dunes.

Over in the Akiti valley, evil King Berserk, Blink-Speed and Yallon rode with a battalion towards the battle. As they crossed into the land of the Feliroo, Mediana's hologram appeared.

"Greetings Your Majesty," said Mediana

"Well witch, have you destroyed those Feliroo vermin?" Berserk asked in anticipation.

"'No, my Lord. we are in the palace now searching for Griscat. Your army is fighting well," Mediana replied.

"Fighting well! What do you mean, witch?" he shouted.

"They are at the Iron Fork, engaging the Feliroo. We have gone ahead to the palace before Griscat escapes,'" said Mediana. She was unaware of what had happened to Skrimp and Porma.

"You should stay with the army at all times. I appointed you to lead them." Berserk was furious.

"Sorry my Lord. I will join them at once."

The hologram disappeared.

"I am surrounded by imbeciles," said Berserk, as he continued his way.

Over on the outskirts of Catabong Palace, King Griscat, Themdar and the rest of the army had reached the Iron Fork - a combined force of Feliroo and Mellow soldiers.

They launched their attack on the risen army of the dead. King Griscat and a small band waited on a nearby hill as Themdar fought her way through to the front of the battle.

Mediana and Luda came out of Catabong Palace and headed for the Iron Fork. The Wand of Nactu lay hidden in a satchel tied to Mediana's waist.

As they drew near to the battle, Luda saw King Griscat waiting on the hill. She pointed in his direction. "The vermin are over there on the hill," she said.

This was the opportunity that they were waiting for.

"Kill him now," ordered Mediana.

Luda circled behind King Griscat and his guards. She got down on all fours, took out a large, jagged knife, and put it between her teeth. Then she crawled stealthily up the hill behind the King.

When she reached the top, she peeped over. King Griscat and his guards were looking the opposite way, engrossed in the battle. Luda took the knife from her mouth and charged at Griscat, stabbing him in the back several times. He fell face first onto the ground, the knife stuck in the middle of his royal cape.

One of his guards immediately speared Luda with a javelin. She lay dying on the floor.

"Griscat is dead. I will go down in history." Luda added with a smile.

"You speak too soon," said the guard.

Luda turned to look at him and her smile disappeared. It was King Griscat in a guard's uniform. He took a javelin and finished Luda off. Now there were only two Special Guard.

The battle intensified with many losses on both sides, but the tide was turning in favour of Berserk's army. They had started to push back the Mellow and Feliroo soldiers. Mediana watched from a distance waiting for Berserk's victory.

Gregory and Placid took Queen Tabatha back to Catabong Palace and left her under the protection of the Mellow Patrol. It was not safe for her to cross the Trubabox because of the Sand Serpent. Once the Queen was safe inside, Gregory and Placid headed to the Iron Fork.

Outside the palace they saw that their army was being overwhelmed by the risen dead soldiers.

"What shall we do?" Gregory asked.

But Captain Placid was not paying attention. She was looking over at a figure, hiding behind a tree.

"That is Mediana," Captain Placid said and drew out her Nid.

"Wait." Gregory commanded.

"Who is Mediana?"

Captain Placid lowered her weapon, "she is Berserk's witch."

"Then we need her alive," said Gregory. He flicked the switch up on the glasses and turned the dial to super-speed. Gregory took a rope out of his backpack, then zoomed over to Mediana and tied her up so tight that she fell to the ground.

"Where is Berserk?" asked Gregory.

Mediana did not respond.

Captain Placid came over "We have no time for this. The battle is almost lost. Let us kill the witch and be done!" she said, before drawing out her Nid once again.

Mediana cowered. "No, don't kill me. I can help you," she begged.

"Where is Berserk?" asked Gregory.

"He is not here," said Mediana.

"The witch lies. The risen soldiers only fight for the one who holds the Nactu," said Placid, raising her weapon.

"I am not lying," said Mediana. "Promise you will spare me, and I will help you."

"I have no time for this nonsense," said Placid.

"No wait," said Gregory. "We will spare you. What do you know?"

"Berserk will soon be here," she said.

"That is no use to us," said Placid as she stepped forward to slay her.

"I have the Nactu," Mediana screamed out in fear.

Placid stopped in her tracks.

"Where is it?"

"It is in my satchel." Mediana nodded towards it as she could not move her hands.

Gregory pulled out the Nactu. "What do I do now?" he asked Placid.

"Command the risen soldiers to stop," she said.

"STOP!" Gregory shouted.

The dead army instantly froze on the spot. Berserk's soldiers also laid down their weapons and surrendered.

King Griscat's army gathered the prisoners of war and forced them to sit around the Iron Fork. Themdar conferred with King Griscat. "What shall we do with them Your Majesty. There are too many for our dungeons."

"Secure their weapons and hold them there for now," said the King.

"Yes, Your Majesty."

Gregory made himself visible, then he and Placid approached King Griscat, dragging Mediana with them.

"Any news of Queen Tabatha?" the King asked, looking concerned.

"She is safe in the palace, Your Majesty."

"Good! What of Berserk?"

"This witch tells us he is on his way here," said Placid pointing at Mediana.

"We have the Nactu," Gregory said, raising it in the air. "We control his army now."

"Excellent, then we shall set a trap for him," said King Griscat. King Berserk and his battalion were a short way off from Catabong Palace.

"Go and see what is happening!' he ordered Blink-Speed. She nodded and shot off towards the Iron Fork while Yallon stayed at Berserk's side.

When she got near the fork, Blink-Speed stopped in shock at the sight of Berserk's army being held as prisoners. As she stood there staring, Blink-Speed was blindsided as Themdar's javelin pierced her chest, knocking her down dead. Now there was only one Special Guard left.

King Berserk was waiting for Blink-Speed to return with a report from the battle. After a while he grew uneasy.

"Something is wrong," he said to Yallon. Before he could answer they heard a mighty noise and looked towards the horizon.

There, high on the hill, was the risen army of the dead marching towards them with their weapons raised. Berserk was horrified.

"Attack them!" he screamed.

Yallon drew his sword and ran at the risen dead soldiers with his forces.

King Berserk leapt off his chariot and made his escape. He went to a supply wagon and ordered the driver to take him back to Korfe Castle. Then he jumped in the back, covered himself up with canvas, hiding like a coward while the wagon trundled along.

Yallon and his soldiers were overwhelmed by the army of the dead. They put up a mighty resistance, but it was useless. Yallon was cut down by a rusty axe and then impaled by a dead warrior's spear. His life slowly trickled away as he lay motionless on the floor. Indeed, that was the end of the not so Special Guard.

King Berserk's wagon ride lasted fifteen minutes before it came to a standstill. The evil ruler fidgeted under the canvas cover, waiting to hear something; but there was complete silence. Impatiently, he stood up and shouted: "Why have you stopped?"

His eyes bulged out of their sockets in fear, and his cover fell to the ground. The wagon was surrounded by his enemies. Gregory, Captain Placid, King Griscat and Themdar were all staring at him. Berserk raised the band of torment in a vain attempt to fight them off.

"Damn you, Fire Head!" he cried, as he shook the band and it started to glow.

Then the inevitable happened. Berserk was hit simultaneously by multiple weapons.

Captain Placid's Nid severed his arm and it dropped off, the band of torment's glow flickering out. Two javelins entered his chest, courtesy of Themdar and King Griscat.

Berserk fell and lay close to death.

Gregory took something out of his pocket.

"This is for Win," he said and put it in Berserk's mouth. It was a bunch of the small white leaves taken from the Tree of Death. King Berserk cried out in extreme pain and withered away to dust right before their eyes.

"He lived without mercy and died without mercy," said King Griscat, and with that they all left to return to their homes.

On the way back to the mountain city Gregory told Placid what had happened to Win. His heart was drenched in pain as he spoke about her.

Once they drew near to the mountain the whole of the Mellow nation were outside celebrating. They were singing and dancing with glee. When they saw Gregory and Placid, the Mellows cheered even louder. Some thirds picked up Gregory and carried him jubilantly in the air to King Cordial.

"Well done, Fire Head," the King said with a warm smile.

"No problem," said Gregory. Then out of the corner of his eye he saw Private Tranquil, Win's mother, standing behind the King. Gregory bowed his head in shame at not being able to save Win from the Snagon.

"What's wrong?" King Cordial asked.

"Excuse me, Your Majesty." Gregory said.

He slowly walked over to Private Tranquil.

"I am so sorry," he said.

"Sorry for what? You saved our nation," said Tranquil.

"About Win' he said softly, his voice cracking with emotion.

"What? I cannot hear you. There is too much noise," said the Private.

"Win," he said loudly.

"Oh, Win. She is here somewhere," Tranquil said, looking around the crowd. "There she is, over there."

Gregory looked over at the crowd. Win was very much alive, and looking as beautiful as ever. His heart flipped when he saw her, and he ran over to hug her tightly.

"I thought you were dead. How did you escape from the Snagon?" he asked with a broad smile.

Win took out a lighter from her pocket and flicked it.

"Don't you remember you gave this to me?" she smiled. "I told you that I can take care of myself."

They laughed and joked celebrating the great victory.

"We will soon go back to Korfe Castle. The Kingdom of Mellow," said Win.

"What will happen to the mountain city?" asked Gregory.

"It will be used as it was before the war. As a training ground for the Mellow Patrol and the sacred garden of fruitful knowledge,"

"Oh, yes, I see," Gregory replied. And this time he truly did. He felt a drop of water on his face. "It is starting to rain," said Gregory.

"The magra is here," Win said looking up, as the rain started to fall heavily.

The Mellows all began to cheer loudly.

"Shall we go inside?" Gregory asked.

Win looked at him strangely.

"The magra brings life," she said. With that carried on dancing.

Gregory watched Win dance with her mother as the Mellows celebrated the return of the magra. He was so glad that she was still alive.

Then suddenly everything became blurry, and Gregory rubbed his eyes. The people of Mellow merged. They became a mega multi-coloured ball that grew bigger and bigger, until it exploded into a million fragments of colour.

WOW! Once again, he was in the book ascending a star-spangled spiral cylinder. The sound of rapid drums and loud bells were ding-donging in his ears. His heart palpitated like a techno tempo.

Gregory was on his way home. *Zoom, Zoom, Zoom.* He was speeding like a motorbike. Then, quicker than you can say 'light-speed', he landed with a '*THUD*' on his bed.

He sat there for a moment trying to gather his thoughts. The book was still in his hands. Gregory went and looked at his calendar. It was the same date as when he had left. "Was it all a dream?" he asked out loud.

"I hope not," said Wedger, popping his head out of the backpack.

"What the heck, Wedger! What are you doing here?"

Gregory could not believe it.

"I'm gonna keep you out of trouble, Fire Head. You know that you won't make it without the Wedger. Just be honest with yourself."

"Hang on a second, Wedger."

Gregory took off the magic glasses. "Now say something."

"You are one ugly Fire Head," said Wedger.

"I can understand you without the glasses."

"That's good. I have educated you. No charge. Welcome to the Wedger school of knowledge."

Gregory picked him up and held him close to his face. "Wedger, I am glad to have you with me, my friend."

"Glad to be here. Who's that over there?" Wedger pointed at the fish tank.

"That's Sharky."

"Can I eat him?"

"No." Gregory choked back his laughter.

"Are you sure?" Wedger raised his orange eyebrow.

"I am sure, Wedger."

Gregory went over to the bookshelf and took another new book. He sat down on the bed and read the title. It was called '*The Rise and Fall of Pompei*'.

"Wedger?"

"Yes, Fire Head."

"Do you like Romans?"

Captain Placid

Gregory

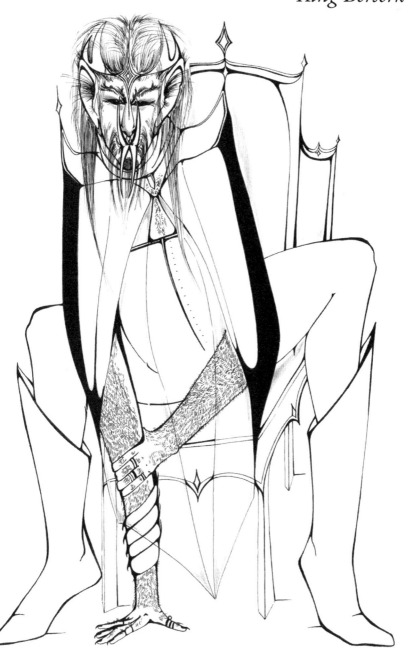

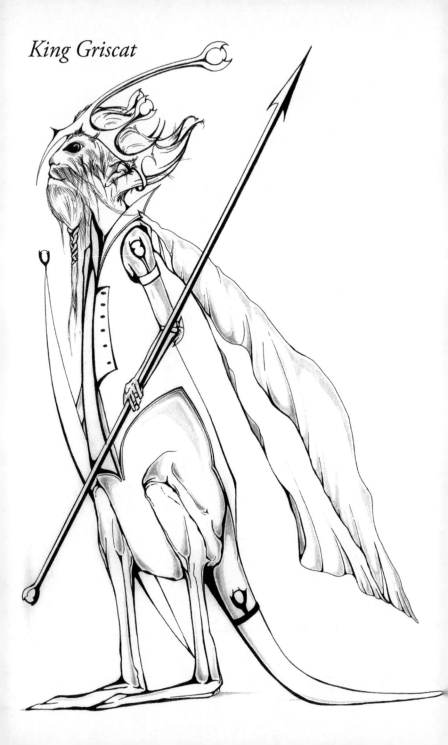

King Griscat

Manaso

Sand Serpant

Skrimp

Wedger

Win